COL...

CHARLES BUTLER

B⊞XTREE

First published in the UK 1992
by BOXTREE LIMITED, 36 Tavistock Street,
London WC2E 7PB

1 3 5 7 9 10 8 6 4 2

ISBN: 1 85283 699 7

Typeset by DP Photosetting,
Aylesbury, Bucks

Printed and bound in Great Britain by
Cox & Wyman Ltd., Reading, Berkshire

A catalogue record for this book is available from the
British Library

Chapter One

The great city of Los Angeles lay blotted out and gasping under a grey gritty blanket of smog. On the streets the air was a warm, eye-watering fug of barely diluted carbon monoxide mixed with a poisonous salt tang, as though the whole Pacific had turned overnight into a cauldron of toxic waste.

It was the kind of day that makes the City's ten million inhabitants even more jumpy and on edge than usual. The kind of day that makes the sleepiest tabby cat suddenly scratch its mistress in the eye; or drives a bishop to kick a hole in a stained glass window. A day when the Precinct Houses batten down the hatches and get ready for more than the usual dose of murder and mayhem. Random killings, robbery, beatings, rape – you name it. Another pretty routine day along California's oceanside paradise.

Murder and mayhem ... Mischief, fraud; sad little family feuds; quarrels, resentments, petty grievances and imagined wrongs: all ripe for law-suit and counter-suit. Grist for the legal mills. It was all in the day's work.

*

In the offices of McKenzie Brackman and Partners, attorneys-at-law, shielded by double-glazed windows and with the metallic air-conditioning on full, they had their own problems too. But even closer to home.

Leland McKenzie, the Senior Partner, was ensconced with Douglas Brackman in Leland's plain but comfortable office. A steamy night had at last fallen outside and the atmosphere in the little room was gloomy.

'Leland, we just have to face reality. When Victor and Michael left, litigation fell off badly. When Jack Sollers went, it nose-dived. And now Abby's going and taking more business with her.'

Leland sat for a moment in silence. He looked tired and old. Brackman had noticed that since the tragic death of Rosalind Shays his partner had seemed to decline visibly – as though the life had gone out of him, along with Rosalind's, so that he was now only firing on two cylinders, if that. But Douglas Brackman loyally kept his observations to himself.

The old man opposite sighed at last, and said, 'All right. The situation is serious. But not yet critical.'

'I disagree,' Brackman said, in his best company voice. 'In three months we've lost four major corporate clients – including the Tammon Group. The bank is so nervous they're even reviewing our line of credit . . .'

'Ridiculous!' Leland snapped, with uncharacteristic vehemence. 'They're overreacting, for Chrissake . . .!'

Brackman shook his head. 'It gets worse. I got a letter today from Parry Littlefield. Because of the Shays claim, Ballantine is doubling our liability premium. And because

2

of Ann Kelsey's suspension, malpractice is going up to half a million.'

'Over my dead body,' Leland growled. 'We'll take our business elsewhere. I'll make a goddam loan if I have to!'

Brackman looked at him grimly. He reminded Leland McKenzie of a well-shaven biblical prophet spelling out the laws from a tablet of stone. 'No, Leland. You can't keep on propping up the firm with Rosalind's money. We just have to consider alternatives.'

Leland sat up straight and brought his hand down with a smack on the table. The suddenness of the gesture startled even the lugubrious Brackman. 'What I will *not* consider, Douglas, is renting space to Susan Bloom!'

Brackman stared at the Senior Partner from under his high-domed forehead. His voice was quiet and emphatic: 'Her practice is phenomenal, Leland. She represents half of Hollywood. And she's prepared to pay top dollar.'

'They call her "Jaws", Douglas,' Leland said, without humour.

Brackman replied in a curious, husky voice that was almost a whisper: 'Just a rumour. Printed in the same rag that called me "a bald bore".'

'Susan Bloom is everything I hate about entertainment law,' Leland went on, with unaccustomed passion. 'She's cheap. She's phony. And she's utterly devoid of ethics.'

Brackman had lowered his head across the table and now really was whispering: '*Shhh!* You don't even know her. I tell you – she's dynamic, she's cutting edge, she's a litigator anyone would be proud to share space with . . .'

'Why are you whispering, Douglas?'

Brackman's head was down, his voice almost inaudible.

3

'She's in my office. She's taken the trouble to stop by on her way to a very important screening.'

'Bloom is *here*?' Leland cried, genuinely aghast. '*Now?*'

Brackman said softly, 'Just meet here. That's all I ask.'

Wearily, and with marked lack of enthusiasm, Leland followed Douglas out into the silent corridor and along to Brackman's austere but elegant office.

*

The woman was sitting in Brackman's high leather chair, her stockinged feet up on his black leather-topped desk, and she was calmly leafing through one of his files. She wore a shapeless neon kaftan down to her ankles, which were the size of billard table legs, and she was slowly drawing on a cigarette that smelt as sweet as a Turkish harem.

Leland McKenzie stopped in the doorway and gave his partner a looked of naked horror. Brackman pretended to ignore it; instead he advanced towards his desk, adjusting a smile that was as thin and phony as the gold on a weekend wedding-ring. 'Susan Bloom?' – he waved his arm expansively towards his Senior Partner – 'Leland McKenzie.'

'Hiya, Leland! I hear you need someone to save your ass!'

It was even worse than Leland expected. The woman in Brackman's chair grinned at him with a mouth like a red letterbox. She was what the more polite Society writers describe as 'stout'; what police dossiers term 'well-nourished'; and what doctors call 'obese'. In fact, she was fat, immensely fat, and very short. Her face, however, in a bad light might have passed as quite pretty – if you liked a woman as hard as a baseball bat, with a jaw like the prow

4

of a speedboat. But now, even in the low generous light from the desk lamp, the usually phlegmatic Leland could not help thinking that it was the sort of face that wouldn't be made-up in the morning – it would be *honed*.

'Okay fellas!' she cried, waving her cigarette at them. 'Sit down and let's talk turkey!'

Brackman sat down opposite her in the client's chair, while Leland looked round helplessly. The only other chair was an upright one against the wall. He walked slowly over and sat down. He was too shocked to feel real anger. That would come later – when the damage was already done.

*

Next day the smog was even more foul: the Pacific daylight reduced to a premature yellow twilight. With Morning Conference over, Leland McKenzie – still smarting from last night's encounter in Brackman's office – returned to his room to find Grace Van Owen standing erect and motionless in front of his desk. Her face was as beautiful as ever, but there was a wounded look in her deep grey eyes.

'Grace!' – he half smiled at her – 'Good to see you!'

'You, too, Leland.' She unclasped her hands in front of her. 'I know I should have made an appointment.'

'Don't be silly,' McKenzie chuckled. As Senior Partner he prided himself on keeping everyone below him at their ease. 'Sit down.' He waved her into the client's chair and sat down himself behind his imposing desk. There was a small pause. For a brief moment he looked uncomfortable. 'I'm so sorry about the baby, Grace.'

'I got your note. Thanks.'

'How's Victor?' McKenzie asked hurriedly.

'Victor and I . . .' Her voice faltered for just a second. 'Victor and I are separated. I'm not practising with him or Michael any more.'

McKenzie stared blankly at her over his bifocals. 'I don't know what to say,' he murmured.

'I'd rather not talk about it,' she said. 'I'm here because I took the Chandler case with me. We empanel today and I can't conduct an effective defence out of my house. I'd like to move in here temporarily and pay you a percentage.'

Leland McKenzie eyed her for a long moment across the desk. 'Grace, this has all happened pretty quickly' – his voice was slow, gentle – 'and you've had a lot to deal with. Maybe you should move for a continuance?'

'I've had two already,' she said. 'Meanwhile, Elsa Chandler's being tried in the Press – the "Ice Queen" who killed her husband. The judge won't agree to another delay.'

'But surely – just a couple of weeks?'

'No.' Grace sat stiffly in her chair, and there was a slight edge in her voice now. 'The D.A. would fight it, too. I'm up against the wall, Leland.'

Leland McKenzie pursed his lips. 'Yes, I see.' He sat for a moment in thoughtful silence. He was a good, decent man and he hated to see this beautiful, brilliant girl – for so long a member of the team, once a judge – so cast down, so brave in her unhappiness. She needed help, he thought. She needed all the help and reassurance he could give.

'You know,' he said at last, 'we could use your name on our letterhead just now. What do you say to coming back to the firm – as Counsel?'

A faint shade of colour rose across her pale face. 'After the way I left . . .? That's mighty generous.'

6

McKenzie gave a modest shrug. 'Not at all. It benefits both of us. You're bringing in something high profile, and we can supply a second chair.'

'I'm not sure it's necessary.'

McKenzie waved the remark aside. 'I insist, Grace. This is a capital case – you'll need someone. It's the very least we can do.'

*

Elsa Chandler was a handsome, elegantly-dressed fake-blonde, still the right side of fifty, with the sort of face and body that made you think she could look after herself. And that was exactly what she was now going to have to do. She was in one of the small witness rooms of the Los Angeles Criminal Courthouse, flanked by Grace Van Owen and Tommy Mullaney, while they prepared her before she stepped outside and braved the pack of snarling Press who waited like wolves in the corridor. Mullaney had placed his hand firmly on her arm, while Grace was taking a last glance inside the folder containing their client's opening statement.

Mullaney's rugged, kindly face crinkled into a smile of bluff reassurance. 'If they get in your way, just stop. We'll do the talking.'

Elsa Chandler swallowed hard. 'I can stand everything but the cameras.' Her voice was low, husky.

'I know,' said Mullaney, 'but they got a right to be here. Just look pleasant and don't smile too big. We'll get you in court as fast as we can.'

'I'm sorry to be a pain, Mr Mullaney. You've been very kind.'

Grace snapped the folder shut and said to Elsa, 'Are you ready?'

'No. But let's go, anyway.'

The three of them stepped out into the big, panelled corridor where the seething scrum of faces moved forward to meet them. Blinding, white lights flashed all around. Half a dozen microphones were thrust into the woman's face like spears. Hard, aggressive voices barked at her from all sides:

'*Mrs Chandler, how does it feel to shoot your husband . . .?*' '*The prosecution seems very confident. Is there a reason . . .?*' '*Did he beg for mercy, Mrs Chandler . . .?*' '*Hey Grace – does being an ex-D.A. give you edge . . .?*'

Elsa Chandler's face, stark and shiny under the merciless glare of the flashes and TV arc-lights, seemed for a moment frozen, while Mullaney thrust his long rangy body in front of her, protecting her as best he could. But still the barrage kept up, brutal and relentless:

'*Is it true your husband's business is worth over ten million dollars, Mrs Chandler . . .?*' '*Given the facts, how optimistic can your client be . . .?*'

This last question was spat at Grace from barely a couple of inches from her face. She replied, in a clear, cool voice, as she continued to elbow her way through the crowd: 'This is a burning bed case – one of long-term abuse.' She didn't hesitate once – hardly even blinked at the continuous flashes all round. 'We're confident Mrs Chandler will be found not guilty.'

She had reached the doors to the courtroom, with Mullaney still managing to shield Mrs Elsa Chandler from the mob of reporters and cameramen. Grace Van Owen drew in a deep breath and steadied herself, before taking her place beside her client. This was the antidote, she thought:

the only way she knew of sloughing off her burden of grief. To have lost Victor – well that was hell, of course, but it was a hell that could be managed and overcome. Their stillborn child was something else . . .

Work – a really tough, daunting case requiring all the skill and quick-witted ingenuity of which she was capable – was the only paliative. The only way she could hope to survive and pull through.

*

The courtroom was packed – standing-room only, even on some of the Press benches. This was going to be one of the biggest murder trials to hit the West Coast in a decade, and the participants were all determined to make the best of it.

Presiding Judge Walter Green sat shrouded in his black gown like an old owl, while the State prosecutor, Assistant Deputy Attorney Bill Graphia – a tall saturnine man with the profile of a 1930's matinee idol – stood swelling up inside his two thousand dollar suit, three tips of white handkerchief adorning his breast pocket, already turning to show his best side to the cameras.

He had a fine, modulated voice like an actor's, and he used it to full effect:

'Elsa Chandler is a murderer,' he began. An icy pause. 'She put a gun in her purse, she took it to her husband's office – and she killed him with it. It was *not* self-defence. It was *not* the desperate act of an abused wife. The evidence will show that it was a well-planned, cold-blooded execution, carried out so that Elsa Chandler could inherit her husband's multi-million dollar estate. It was murder for financial gain. Murder committed solely for the purpose of making Mrs Chandler a rich woman.'

The person at whom this didactic venom was directed sat between Grace Van Owen and Tommy Mullaney, as still as a marble bust. No expression, no hint of emotion crossed her firm, well-sculptured features. Graphia's voice cut through the silence like a knife:

'When you hear the facts, members of the jury, when you weigh the evidence – you will reach the only possible conclusion: that Elsa Chandler is guilty of murder with special circumstances, beyond a reasonable doubt.' He inclined his body in a slight bow. 'Thank you.'

As he sat down, Grace Van Owen rose, nodded to the Judge, then turned to the jury box. Her face was calm, her voice measured: 'Ralph Chandler battered his wife for twelve years.' The silence was total – not even a scratch, a cough, a shuffle. She didn't have to raise her voice a single octave.

'A number of times, including the morning of his death, Ralph Chandler forcibly raped his wife. I'm not talking about a wife reluctant to make love to an insistent husband. I'm talking about violent, brutal, forced sex. I'm talking about a husband who had to control his wife's every move – a husband who was aroused by humiliating her.' Grace paused, just long enough to steady her breathing.

'This was the man Elsa Chandler shot in self-defence. A man who tortured her for twelve years – whose abuse she couldn't endure or survive any longer. Ralph Chandler swore he would kill his wife that night, ladies and gentlemen. She took the gun with her to his office that day because she believed him.'

The atmosphere in the courtroom remained as taut as

piano wire. Even the rows of slick, hard-boiled crime reporters were listening with lips parted, as though mesmerised. Grace was the best-looking young attorney on the West Coast – and she was sure worth listening to, as well!

*

She didn't show it, but when that first day of the trial was finally adjourned, Grace Van Owen was whacked – played out, utterly exhausted. That evening she had started wearily to unpack some of her things in her new office. There was a faint tap at the door. It was Leland McKenzie. He gave her a diffident smile. 'Grace? – got a minute?'

'For you, Leland, I have five!' She straightened and smiled back.

McKenzie closed the door. 'I wanted to tell you how happy I am to have you aboard again.'

'It's mutual, Leland.'

The old man hesitated. Perhaps he could see the lines of deep tiredness round her mouth; he was embarrassed, intruding on her like this after this first harrowing day in court, but hc was a good man, and he needed to talk to her. It wasn't just a matter of routine politeness. It was his duty.

'Grace, I know you and Victor are none of my business. But if there's anything I can do . . .'

'I'm fine, Leland. Really I am.' Her smile was only half forced.

Leland looked awkward, fumbling for the next words. 'When Rosalind and I . . . er, when I lost her – well, I thought I was fine. Went about my business – in control –

no problem. But there was no joy, Grace. I was just going through the motions.'

'I'm sorry, Leland.' Her face had grown slack with exhaustion. 'It's been kind of a long day.'

'Of course!' he said hurriedly. 'I should let you get back to work.' He paused, his hand on the doorknob. 'I'm here if you need me. Goodnight.'

'Goodnight.' She watched the door close, the muscles in her face grown taut with the effort of fighting back the tears; then, having won the battle, she returned briskly to her unpacking.

Chapter Two

*

The prosecution's first witness next day was Detective Tom Blomquist, a heavy, grizzled man in his fifties, with that hard, slightly battered look of a man who has seen everything and is not easily thrown. He gave his evidence stolidly, with as much emotion as if he were reading a laundry list.

'So,' said A.D.A. Graphia, 'Mrs Chandler called and asked you to come to Ralph Chandler's office. What did you find when you got there, Detective?'

'Mr Chandler's body was face-down on the floor, by the desk.' Blomquist spoke without notes. 'There was a gunshot wound in his chest. Mrs Chandler was sitting in a chair beside the body. She was holding a .38-calibre handgun.'

'Did she tell you whose it was?'

'She said it was hers – she'd brought it from home. The gun was registered to her husband.'

'When you first saw her, did Mrs Chandler seem upset? Was she crying?'

'No. She was real calm – real quiet.'

Graphia inclined his sleek dark head towards the jury box, as though to indicate: *I told you so!* – then back to the detective: 'And what did Mrs Chandler say, when you found her beside her husband's body?'

'She said Ralph Chandler deserved to die – and that she'd killed him.'

Graphia just nodded, turned to the Judge and said, 'I have no more questions.'

*

It was now Grace's turn. She sounded as crisp and fresh as the folded handkerchief in Graphia's breast pocket. She never once raised her voice:

'Detective Blomquist, did it appear to you that Mrs Chandler was in shock?'

Graphia was on his feet again: '*Objection!* Witness isn't qualified to make that judgement.'

Grace had turned to the Judge. 'He's been a police officer for twenty-five years. He's seen all kinds of people, in all kinds of situations, react to trauma.'

The Judge nodded. 'Overruled.'

'You've seen shock look like extreme composure, haven't you, Detective?' Grace continued. 'The same composure Mrs Chandler showed the night of her husband's death?'

Detective Blomquist's head dropped a fraction. 'Yes.'

'And she had good reason to be in shock, hadn't she?'

The policeman shrugged. 'I have no idea.'

'You took a statement from Mrs Chandler.' Grace's voice had taken on a slight edge. 'Didn't she tell you her marriage was a nightmare? Didn't she say her husband forced her to come to his office that night? And didn't she tell you *exactly* why she killed him?'

'Yeah – she said he raped her. But not that night.'

14

Grace moved in quickly: 'But didn't she tell you he *had* raped her – as recently as that morning? And had physically abused her for twelve years? That he'd burned her with cigarettes – had held her head under water . . .?'

Graphia was up again: '*Objection!*'

'Overruled.' Judge Green sounded almost bored.

Grace gave a little nod of acknowledgement. She turned again to the policeman: 'Didn't she say those things, Detective?'

Blomquist hesitated. 'Yes, but . . .'

'And didn't Mrs Chandler tell you how terrified she was of her husband?' Grace had Blomquist in her sights now. 'How, when he ordered her to his office, she became frantic? That she was afraid if she went, he'd kill her? And if she didn't, he'd come home and do it there?'

Blomquist was groping for words, 'That was her story – yeah . . .'

'Didn't she say that if she ran – if she hid – he'd find her? That *that* was why she found her husband's gun and took it to the office? Because she didn't know what else to do? Wasn't that also part of Mrs Chandler's statement to you?'

Detective Blomquist looked resigned. 'Yes.'

'Thank you, Detective.' Grace sat down, to a faint murmur of approval from the public benches behind her.

A.D.A. Graphia now rose again. He seemed less assured this time, sensing that Grace had won that last round. He looked determined to equalise. He faced Blomquist with his best prosecutor's glare:

'Did you see any evidence of abuse that night? Was Mrs Chandler's clothing torn? Did she have any bruises or broken bones? Were there any signs of a struggle in her husband's office?'

'No,' the detective said. 'Nothing like that. Just the body on the floor.'

Graphia nodded and sat down, satisfied he had made a quick cross-cut to dent Grace's vivid portrait of the distraught, battered wife.

*

Later in the day Graphia had a more dangerous witness up on the stand. Sandra Vosburgh was an accountant in her late fifties – a lean blondish woman with the angular, drawn features that come from too much experimental dieting, and the dull eyes of a 'girl' who looks back too often at her lost youth. Her elaborate hair was obviously not her own. On the stand she appeared almost expressionless, but on the rail her knuckles showed white.

'What happened when you went to the Chandlers' home a week before Mr Chandler was killed?' Graphia asked her smoothly.

Grace leapt to her feet. 'Your Honour, I renew my objection to this witness . . .'

'Overruled. Witness will answer,' growled Judge Green.

Sandra Vosburgh cleared her throat. 'I went there to go over a tax problem. When I arrived, Ralph and Elsa were arguing.'

'Violently?'

'Oh, no. Ralph never raised his voice but he was pretty upset. Elsa had written twenty thousand dollars' worth of cheques on their joint account.'

'Who were the cheques made out to?' Graphia said eagerly.

16

'Some were for cash. The rest were made out to Waering Antiques.'

Graphia raised his eyebrows. 'Ms Vosburgh, did Mrs Chandler tell her husband what the money was for?'

'She said she bought a Chinese vase and some paintings – but Ralph didn't believe her.'

Graphia returned to his seat and Grace came forward.

'Ms Vosburgh, you said it was a joint account. So, technically, didn't the money belong to both of them?'

'Yes, but Ralph never liked Elsa to write cheques unless he approved.'

'In other words, he wanted total control.' Grace's voice was deliberate, emphasising each word.

Sandra Vosburgh looked embarrassed but reluctantly agreed.

'When Mrs Chandler told her husband about the Chinese vase, what did he do?' Grace stared defiantly at Sandra Vosburgh, who was looking increasingly uncomfortable and remained silent. Grace continued: 'He took a hammer and – what did he do, Ms Vosburgh?'

Sandra Vosburgh's hands were tightly clenched; she was breathing hard. 'He destroyed the vase,' she said at last.

Grace looked around the courtroom, her eyes finally resting on the judge. 'Thank you. Nothing further.'

The next witness to be called was Steven Waering. Immediately, Grace leapt to her feet again. 'Objection. Witness is not on the list. What possible relevance could he . . .'

Graphia interrupted: 'In the past twenty-four hours, we've discovered an intimate relationship between Mr Waering and the defendant . . .'

'Objection!' Grace cried. 'Your Honour, this is a blatant attempt to blindside the defence. I move to exclude . . .'

Judge Green sighed. 'Take it easy, Ms Van Owen. If Mr Graphia didn't know about the witness, he didn't know. He will provide you with his investigative reports. To be fair to your client, I'll give you till tomorrow afternoon.'

'It's not enough!' Grace said vehemently.

'In my opinion, it is.' The judge's face was set.

'Then I move for a stay, Your Honour. I want time to get a writ on that ruling from the Court of Appeals . . .'

Mullaney nudged her. 'Don't do this,' he said quietly.

Judge Green puffed himself up like a toad. 'You've got to be kidding,' he said to Grace. 'They'd throw you out on your ear.' Grace began to object again. 'I've ruled,' the Judge said firmly. 'We're adjourned.' He rose to his feet and swept out of the courtroom, looking extremely annoyed.

Tommy Mullaney gave Grace a slow sideways glance from under his untidy grey–blond hair. 'Let's take a deep breath, honey,' he murmured. 'Okay . . .?'

*

Tommy Mullaney still had his arm round her shoulders, but she shook him off as they walked into the panelled witness room where Elsa Chandler was already seated at the bare wooden table. Tommy followed, with his slow, slightly slouching gait.

As soon as the woman saw them both, she started talking as though a pent-up flood of words were pouring over a broken dam:

'I met him at a charity auction. Ralph would sometimes let me go to those without him. Steven and I had lunch –

nothing illegal about that, is there? We got to be friends.' She paused, with a look of feeble defiance – a defiance that masked intense nervousness. For she had every reason to be nervous. Grace Van Owen's face was like stone. Tommy Mullaney looked less threatening.

'But that wasn't all,' Grace said, her voice low, icy.

Mullaney was stirring some pages from the file in front of him. 'The D.A. says you spent the night with Waering. They got the security video from his garage. You came in at 1.04 a.m. and you left at 6.15. This was three months before your husband was killed.'

Elsa Chandler's face had suddenly become frantic. 'Ralph got drunk that night! When he drank, he liked to play a game which he called . . . *How Should I Kill Elsa?*' She drew in her breath sharply, almost a sob, then put her head in her hands. She began speaking in short, halting gasps: 'He would say . . . "*Shall I beat her to death? . . . Should I cut her throat? . . . Maybe I should strangle her . . .*"' She broke off, looking imploringly at each of them.

'It went on for hours, until he passed out. I *had* to talk to somebody. Steven said I could call him any time. I finally got to the phone and could hardly speak, I was so upset. Steven said I should get away from home, come to his apartment in case Ralph woke while he was still drunk and carried out his threat. I was desperate – I *had* to get away.

Grace spoke very quietly: 'So you went to Steven's apartment and slept with him.'

Elsa Chandler looked at each of them, her pallor had drained away – she had gone very red. '*No!*' – she almost screamed the word at them both – 'We only talked! He tried to get me to leave my husband but I couldn't. I still thought Ralph needed me. After a few hours, I got scared that he'd wake up with a hangover and find me gone. So I went home. He never threatened to kill me when he was sober. I didn't sleep with Steven – and that's the truth.' Her voice choked and trailed off into a sob.

Grace and Tommy exchanged brief glances, then turned again to their distraught client.

'That's still going to be hard for the jury to swallow,' Tommy said gently.

'It's none of their business!' Elsa banged her fist on the table, then, with an obvious effort to control herself, went on, 'Steven is the only good thing in my life. Ralph made me think I could never love anyone. Steven changed that. I was beginning to . . . *feel* . . . and I hadn't had any feelings for so long.'

Grace nodded. 'If the jury realises you're in love with Steven, they're going to believe the Prosecution,' she said, then paused, before delivering the knock-out. 'You'll probably go to the gas chamber.'

Tommy Mullaney looked quickly at her, slightly shocked. 'Take it easy . . .' he began; but Grace kept on, twisting the knife in the wound:

'The jury won't see you as an abused wife who defended herself against a habitual rapist. They'll think of you as a cheating bitch who killed her husband for money.'

Tommy kicked her ankle under the table. 'I think you made your point,' he muttered.

Tears were now rolling down Elsa Chandler's cheeks but Grace wouldn't let go. 'Not telling us about Steven Waering was a lie. If you lie to us again, we drop the case.' And Grace stood up and marched out of the room; Tommy followed, with a backward glace of sympathy for the stricken woman.

*

Back in the office, Grace sat behind her desk looking nervous and defensive. Across the room Tommy Mullaney lounged in the clients' chair. 'I talked to a friend and two guys Steven Waering works with,' he drawled. 'Seems the guy's OK. Divorced – loves his kids – doesn't fool around.'

'But his child support is always late and his business is in deep trouble,' Grace said bitterly. The discovery of Waering threatened to be a disaster.

'OK,' Tommy sighed, 'it's not going to be a picnic. Maybe I should take over. The judge is probably still mad at you.'

'Come on,' said Grace. 'I had to hit back.'

'Sure, but not with the Court of Appeals! You lost your temper.'

'I had every right. They were walking all over us.'

'Elsa Chandler wasn't.' Tommy's voice was soft, almost laconic; only his words conveyed urgency: 'She made a mistake – sure. But you didn't have to slap her around like that. You scared the hell out of her! That's what her husband did and it made her shut down emotionally. If she does that on the witness stand, we're dead.'

Grace was suddenly truculent, furious. 'I don't have time for this, Tommy! I have to be ready for Waering in two hours.' And abruptly, ostentatiously, she began looking through Graphia's file.

Tommy spoke very quietly, knowing he was walking on broken glass. 'Grace, this isn't like you. You've been overdoing it. Take a break. Let me question Waering and give Judge Green a chance to cool off.'

Defiantly, Grace said, 'It's my call. I can handle it. Just be there to back me up.'

Chapter Three

Next morning, Graphia had Steven Waering on the stand. He was a well-built, greying man with a deep suntan, dressed in casual clothes that must have cost what a maintenance-man earns in two months. On first inspection, a routine specimen hunk of Californian home-wrecking beefcake. Or so Grace had thought. So had Graphia. Grace had been prepared to hate the man on sight, but very soon she was to revise her opinion of the witness.

For the moment the A.D.A. had the beefcake all to himself. The two of them made a handsome pair, Grace thought bitchily, they ought to try the movies together.

'Once more, Mr Waering,' Graphia was saying, 'Mrs Chandler visited your apartment regularly . . .'

'Three times, over eight months,' the man on the stand answered smoothly.

'And at least one of those times, she spent the night with you?'

'Not the way you mean – no.' The words were spoken with no particular emphasis – only matter-of-factly – but their effect was like a grenade being thrown in the courtroom.

Graphia gulped, as though he'd just swallowed half a tiara, but the greatest effect was on Grace – though she managed to conceal it with extraordinary willpower. She was suddenly uplifted, and began looking more closely at Mr Steven Waering, wondering how she could have misjudged the man so badly. Or had she? Middle-aged studs like him didn't usually gainsay their amorous triumphs – *surely*?

Graphia, too, was staring nonplussed at his surprise witness, but he recovered quickly from Waering's shock-answer, and his line of questioning smoothly changed gear:

'An attractive woman – who loves you – comes to your apartment at 1 a.m. – stays till dawn . . . *And you don't sleep with her?*' His saturnine features had assumed a standard-issue mask of disdainful irony.

'Objection!' said Grace. 'He's badgering.'

'Witness is hostile,' Graphia snarled.

'Overruled,' said Judge Green.

Graphia was now looking Steven Waering hard in the eye. 'Are you *denying* you had a sexual relationship with Elsa Chandler before her husband was killed?'

'Yes. We were friends, I was trying to help her . . .' Waering began.

'Help her leave her marriage?' Graphia said, with a visible curling of the lip, in the best ham-theatrical tradition. 'Help her funnel Ralph Chandler's money into your failing business . . .?'

Grace was back on her feet. 'Objection!'

'Sustained,' said Green.

Suddenly Waering got angry. He stood with both hands gripping the rail of the stand, his handsome features tightening with intensity, the suntan turned a shade paler. 'He was beating her, for God's sake! He was *raping* her!'

'According to *her*,' Graphia sneered. 'But the truth was, Elsa Chandler desperately wanted to get rid of her husband, so she could be with you.'

'No!' Waering shouted, and Grace chimed in. 'Objection!'

'She had to get *out* . . .!' Waering yelled, really angry now.

'She *wanted* out because of you!' Graphia responded triumphantly. 'And you needed the cash.'

'*We* weren't the criminals,' Waering said in desperation. 'He was . . .!'

'No further questions,' Graphia said, and resumed his seat.

But Waering wasn't going to be left high and dry. 'The way he treated her – it was *psychotic!*' he cried, looking at the jury imploringly, then at the judge. 'What happened to Ralph Chandler was his own fault!'

'That'll do, Mr Waering,' the judge warned.

As he spoke, Tommy Mullaney leant over and murmured to Grace, 'They're not so sure about him. We gotta build up sympathy fast.'

Grace showed no expression as she rose and faced the witness. Steven Waering looked confused and still very angry. 'You knew Elsa Chandler was married, didn't you, Mr Waering?'

'Yes. She told me when we first met. But she didn't tell me the kind of monster she was married to.'

Graphia sprang up, 'Objection – non-responsive. Move to strike.'

'Jury will disregard the answer,' Judge Green said wearily.

'When did you realise Elsa Chandler was being abused by her husband?' said Grace.

Graphia was up again. 'Objection! No foundation – he didn't see any abuse.'

'He was with the defendant right after she was brutalised' – Grace spoke before the Judge could get in his ruling – 'this man is an eye-witness, your Honour.'

'After the fact,' Graphia growled.

Judge Green nodded. 'I'll allow you some latitude on this one, Ms Van Owen. But don't push it.'

'I still object!' Graphia said.

Green glared at him. 'And don't *you* push it, either, Mr Graphia. You'll get your re-direct.'

Grace waited till her opponent had sunk back in his seat. For the first time she thought that dapper, dynamic D.A.A. Bill Graphia was looking worried. She turned again to the witness:

'I repeat, Mr Waering – when did you realise Elsa Chandler was being abused by her husband?'

'The night she came to my apartment at 1 a.m. She was white and shaking. Under her raincoat, her blouse was torn. Her cheek was bruised and she had blood all over her.' Waering hesitated, his voice low and near to cracking. 'There were cuts on her neck and her breasts.'

'Who did she say inflicted those cuts?' Grace asked.

'Ralph Chandler.' Waering paused, then said out loud and clear: 'With a butcher's knife. He did that sometimes before he raped her . . .'

'Objection!' Graphia roared.

'Sustained.'

Grace ignored the interjection. She was sure she had Graphia beat this round – and perhaps for the duration. 'Did Mrs Chandler tell you these things – easily – Mr Waering?'

The witness looked down at his hands, still gripping the rail. 'No. At first she couldn't talk at all. It took hours before she told me what he'd done. When it finally came out, I wanted to kill him myself.'

'Had she ever said anything about her husband before?' Grace asked him.

Steven Waering seemed on the point of tears when he answered, 'She tried so hard not to. I knew something was wrong, but I could never get her to say what. After all the sick things he did to her, she was still loyal . . .'

'Your Honour, please!' Graphia broke in, with pained distaste.

Green nodded. 'Confine yourself to answering the question, Mr Waering.'

Grace went on: 'From what you witnessed that night, Mr Waering – from the physical evidence of what you *saw* – do you have any doubt at all that Elsa Chandler was severely abused?'

Waering was trying to stifle his emotion; the neck muscles under his taut brown skin stood out like ropes under canvas. 'She was bleeding,' he said at last. 'She was terrified. You can't fake that kind of thing.' He took a deep breath. 'Of course she was abused.'

Grace nodded. 'Thank you, Mr Waering.'

Graphia now rose, slowly, with theatrical effect. 'Mr Waering, you don't know that Mrs Chandler was abused by her husband, do you? In fact, you don't actually *know* she was abused by anybody. The truth is, she *could* have faked it.'

'Objection,' said Grace, with restraint; she was determined not to get overheated – it was going too well to risk upsetting again the good Judge Walter Green. But before Green had the chance to rule, Graphia corrected himself:

'I'll rephrase the question.' His voice was as slippery as a bucketful of eels. 'Mr Waering, have you considered that Elsa Chandler could have inflicted what were really minor injuries on herself, in order to gain your sympathy?'

'It's possible. But she didn't.'

Graphia gave an oily smile. 'The two of you are close. Maybe you agreed to back up Mrs Chandler's story? To help her fabricate an excuse for murdering her husband . . .?'

'Objection!' Grace cried.

'Sustained.'

'You're in love with Elsa Chandler, aren't you, Mr Waering?' Graphia said suddenly.

'I don't see what that has to do with . . .!'

'Answer the question, please,' Graphia said. 'Are you in love with Elsa Chandler – yes or no?'

'Yes.'

'Would you lie to save her life?'

'No.'

Graphia kept on at Waering. 'According to phone company records, Ralph Chandler called your store from his office on July 10th, 1990. He asked if his wife was there, didn't he?'

Waering nodded uneasily. 'Yes.'

'And Elsa Chandler *was* there, wasn't she?'

'Yes.'

'Did you tell that to her husband?'

'He'd have gone crazy – he'd have beaten her again . . .!'

'*Did* you tell Ralph Chandler that his wife was there?' Graphia persisted.

'No.'

'So you lied. To protect Mrs Chandler. Yes?'

There was a hush across the courtroom. 'Yes,' Waering said at last. He seemed to have lost two inches in height in as many seconds.

'No further questions,' Graphia said, and sat down, looking quietly satisfied. He had all the answers he needed.

Judge Green adjourned; tomorrow was a public holiday. As the courtroom emptied, Grace and Tommy Mullaney exchanged glances as if to say, the damage is now done. It had been going so well with Waering: then suddenly it had all fallen apart. It was now their turn to look worried. Waering had been hurt, and so had their client.

*

After leaving the courtroom, they'd both headed back to the office and gone into Grace's new room to discuss the case and consider their chances. Neither was too optimistic. Tommy sat sprawled out in the client's chair, managing his remarkable feat of appearing both tense and relaxed at the same time. His voice was a slow, dreamy, tobacco-chewing drawl: 'You were great back there. But the boyfriend hurt us.'

Grace looked drained. 'Well, at least they rest tomorrow. We put Elsa on the stand no later than Thursday.'

Tommy studied the empty ceiling. 'She worries me, Grace. She could get up there and just check out – protect

28

herself so darned much she sounds like the goddam phone book!'

'You can suggest another choice?' Grace said wearily.

Tommy Mullaney raised his hand, stared at his thumb, then stuck it in his ear. 'No. She's the only way to prove abuse. But we gotta hit hard on temporary insanity. He made her do things she'd never have done in cold blood.'

Grace shook her head. 'No! I'm going with self-defence.'

'And insanity,' said Tommy. 'You filed both, remember.'

'I'm not using both. I want a clean acquittal,' she said bluntly.

'The odds are against you. She took the gun *with* her – so we can't prove immediate threat. We gotta have insanity to fall back on. That way it's still not guilty.'

Grace smoothed a hand across her brow. Her eyes were hollow and there were deep shadows of tiredness under them. 'There's been too much publicity already – the judge will have to commit her. She ends up victimised again.'

Tommy sat up in his chair. 'Aw hell, Grace! You don't wanna go for broke here.'

Grace looked at him with a flash of anger. 'I don't want Elsa Chandler rotting in a mental ward – possibly for the rest of her life!'

'Well, at least she'll have a life. With straight self-defence you're taking too much of a gamble.'

Grace flared up with rage: 'Don't you try to second-guess me, Tommy! I know what I'm doing.'

'Yeah – well so do I. You know something, Grace – you're acting out. You've still got a lot of anger in there over the baby, and you're letting it cloud your judgement.' He leant over and put his broad hand over hers, covering it completely. 'As your friend, Grace – I know it's gotta be

29

killing you, and I'm sorry. But I have to say that on behalf of our client, I think it stinks.'

Grace looked firmly back at him; she was still very angry, but also disappointed. She liked Mullaney. 'This was a mistake, Tommy. I see that now. You're just not comfortable, are you, with second chair? I'll ask someone else.'

Tommy sat back. 'Great! Dump me – railroad the client! Do your best to screw things up.' He stood up and pushed his chair hard up against the desk. 'But I'll tell you just one thing for nothing. No matter what happens to Elsa Chandler, what's hurting you is still gonna be there!' And he marched out of the room, closing the door noisily behind him.

Grace sat for some moments without moving. She stared at the empty chair, then stared at her hands, placed neatly in front of her on the black leather desk-top. At first, her face maintained a stiff, formal serenity. Then her head flopped down on to her hands and she began weeping, silently, uncontrollably.

Chapter Four

Leland McKenzie, mercifully oblivious of the suspended drama unfolding in the Criminal Court, or of the growing disharmony between two of his star performers, had spent an uneventful day going through the firm's wilting accounts.

He was now leaving the office, tired and looking forward to a simple supper by himself, followed by the release of sleep. He had got as far as the reception area and was just opening the glass doors at the entrance, when the lift doors opened. McKenzie stopped in his tracks.

Two burly figures in boiler-suits were struggling with an enormous abstract painting which they began edging clumsily out into the hall, bumping and scraping the doors. But this – hideous though it was, to his taste – was not what shocked him. For a third figure now appeared from the lift, strutting heavily into Leland's line of vision. It was Susan Bloom, in a blood-red business suit, with high padded shoulders and a red pageboy's cap set at a raffish angle on her jet-black hair.

To Leland, tired after the day's work, it was like an awful apparition. Momentarily transfixed, he watched the ungainly trio reach the glass doors of the office. He just managed to step aside as the first of the 'rude mechanicals' backed against one of the doors and dealt a sharp blow with the edge of the frame against the glass panel.

'Hey, watch it!' Bloom yelled, in a voice like a power-drill. 'That picture's worth more than this company!' She looked up and saw McKenzie's stricken face. 'Hi Leland baby! I heard on the car radio the Chandler case is reaching boiling point. Like a bet on which way she walks? Free or into the gas chamber?'

'Certainly not,' said Leland. 'I consider the suggestion both insensitive and improper.' His glowering gaze was distracted by the two removal men, who had returned to the elevator and were now heaving out an enormous desk, upright, towards the glass doors. As he stood watching in dismay, Roxanne appeared beside him, also on her way home. She stopped too.

*

'Is she moving in?' she asked, in a stage whisper.

'Regrettably, yes.' Susan Bloom either hadn't heard, or didn't care. McKenzie sighed and looked forlornly at Roxanne. 'Where are you when I need you, Rox?' he said, as they both started towards the lifts.

A brief but explicit obscenity came from behind. Susan Bloom swept past them, caught the lift door before it closed, and came out again, clasping a huge snakeskin handbag. Roxanne rolled her eyes towards the roof of the lift, as she and Leland got in and the door slid shut behind them.

Grace Van Owen was at her desk, surrounded by a neat array of files, foolscap and freshly sharpened pencils, when Ann Kelsey put her head into the office. Grace looked up and smiled brightly. 'Hi!'

'I know it's short notice,' Ann said, 'but Stuart and I would love you to come home with us for dinner.' She put a finger to her lips. 'He's making his killer pasta and I have all the stuff for the Caesar salad . . .'

Grace smiled back but there was no joy in her voice. 'I'd love to, Ann. But not tonight.'

Ann paused. 'You don't have to see Matthew. He'll probably be asleep.'

'I can't. Okay?'

Ann nodded. 'Okay. When you're ready.' At the door she turned. 'We miss you, Grace.'

Grace sat very still and did not reply. The door closed.

*

Dr Adam Carton was a dry spare man, as bald as a scrubbed potato, dressed in an immaculate black suit and stiff, very white cuffs. His manner was slow, grave, with the melancholic integrity of an experienced undertaker. In fact, he was one of the State's leading psychiatrists, and an expert on criminal and deviant behaviour, particularly in relation to sexual violence. His recently published book, *Violence At Home*, was still on the national bestseller lists. Dr Adam Carton might not be showing it – that would have been utterly at variance with the image of medical rectitude that he must maintain at all times – but he was thoroughly enjoying every minute in the limelight.

He was now on the stand in the Los Angeles Criminal Court, appearing as a defence witness in the Elsa Chandler murder case. He answered Grace Van Owen with his most precise, authoritative manner. 'You have to understand,' he was saying, 'that battered women come from all social classes. It's a myth that they're poor and uneducated. Some studies have shown a higher incidence of abuse in places like Bel Air and Beverly Hills.'

Grace listened gravely. She was not only pleased with the doctor's evidence: she was fascinated by it. 'Why don't these people leave, Doctor?' she said, genuinely interested in the answer. Dr Adam Carton paused judiciously. He frowned slightly and folded his neat white hands across his waist. Only the most cynical observer would have said he was acting out before the court, playing to the gallery for all his righteous professionalism was worth.

He cleared his throat before answering. 'Such women think like concentration camp victims. When human beings are subjected to daily terror, to constant punishment – well, options like escape simply cease to exist. These women focus on avoiding the beatings, and when that fails, to surviving them.'

'What if they try to get out?' said Grace.

'Then they're even *more* likely to be attacked by the abusive partner. Special hostels – women's shelters – even the police can't seem to protect them.'

'Dr Carton, is it probable that Mrs Chandler's husband would have continued to abuse her?'

'There's almost no doubt he would. In fact, in my

considered opinion the violence would have become more frequent – more severe.'

Grace nodded, as though the beneficiary of some deep wisdom. 'And in your opinion, Doctor, the night he ordered her to his office, was it reasonable for Elsa Chandler to believe her husband would kill her?'

'Absolutely. With that kind of long-term abuse, Mrs Chandler's life was in danger every time she was alone with him.'

'Thank you, Doctor. I have nothing further.' *Thank you indeed, Doctor!* she thought triumphantly, as she started back to her seat beside Elsa Chandler and Tommy Mullaney. This was the best thing that had happened in the whole trial! More of this and they'd be on to a home-run. She was only puzzled that Assistant Deputy Attorney Graphia hadn't once intervened. It couldn't be because he was overawed by the doctor's professional status. For Bill Graphia held all professions in contempt, except his own.

He now rose, slowly, thoughtfully, examining Dr Adam Carton like a matador appraising a piqued bull for its most vulnerable spot. 'Doctor, aren't these studies you mention largely anec–'

'Your Honour!' – Tommy Mullaney was on his feet with the speed of a released spring, cutting Graphia off mid-word – 'We reserve the right to recall this witness.'

'That won't be necessary,' Grace said decisively, without looking at her colleague.

Tommy, half standing, turned and stared down at her. His voice was soft but urgent. 'We just forget insanity?' he said to her, the words barely audible.

Graphia, delighted by this apparent dissension in the ranks of his opponents, returned to the fray and completed his original question to the expert witness: 'Aren't these studies anecdotal, Doctor?'

'There are hundreds' – Dr Adam Carton stifled a little cough – 'hundreds of case histories . . .'

But the effect of his words were deflected by Grace's loud whisper to Tommy Mullaney beside her: 'I told you. I'm dropping it . . .!'

Mullaney stood up and faced Judge Green: 'Your Honour, I need a ten-minute recess.'

'Granted.'

*

Tommy Mullaney was not easily ruffled or made angry – at least, not visibly so. But just sometimes the mask slipped, and it did so now, as he followed Grace into the witness room and closed the door firmly behind them. Neither of them sat down.

'You said you were thinking about it' – the red gleam of the executioner's axe showed in the corner of his eyes – 'Your last words to me, Grace. *You – were – thinking – about – the insanity plea* . . . Yes?'

'Yes, I was.' Her face was pale, infuriatingly calm. (*God*, Tommy thought, *The nervous energy this girl must burn up in just one hour . . . Enough to run all the lights in all the city buildings in L.A. . . .!*)

His slack jaw had firmed up, his mouth no longer had that loose casual look; he was very angry, and close to despair. 'You're really gonna do this, aren't you? Lose temporary insanity – hang your whole case on self-defence, and hope the jury believes her.'

'Killing her husband,' said Grace, 'was probably the

36

most rational thing Elsa Chandler ever did. She does not belong in a psychiatric ward, Tommy.'

'She shot him before he even laid a hand on her. Grace, you know the law as well as I do. You have to show immediate threat or you don't make self-defence.'

Now it was Grace's turn to get angry. 'He brutalised her for twelve years! He promised to kill her – he *made* her bring him the gun. They just have to see that as immediate threat . . .!'

'Yeah – and what if they don't? They didn't when you prosecuted Reuben Mercato.' He leaned his face closer to hers, urging her, almost pleading with her. 'Grace, listen to what I'm saying. You need Dr Carton's testimony on her state of mind. If you drop it now, you can't bring it back. For God's sake, *get in there and get it on the record . . .*'

She was unmoved. 'This is how I'm trying the case. If you don't like it, Tommy, you can get out.'

His hands hung loosely at his sides. 'Anything you say.' He shrugged and walked out of the room.

*

At Morning Conference next day Stuart Markowitz was exchanging idle chat with no-one in particular about the virtues of king salmon for dinner parties – one of his old law school buddies had apparently just sent him one and he seemed anxious to invite the whole firm, whether separately or together was not clear, in order to sample it. 'Don't worry, Ann will be doing the cooking,' he added, chuckling.

John Castroverti – a recent recruit to the firm – laughed politely: he was ever anxious to oblige, to be one of the team. Grace and Tommy Mullaney exchanged a quick,

37

cool look; they didn't even smile. Nor did Douglas Brackman.

'Settle down, please', Brackman said, fussing with his papers. 'We have a full agenda. Where's Arnold?'

'Getting his allergy shot,' said McKenzie.

'*Ouch!*' said Castroverti, pulling a face of mock-horror, then glancing round for approval. None came.

'First – the Elsa Chandler trial,' Brackman went on.

Grace sat up and brushed an invisible hair out of her eyes. 'Tomorrow I have one witness to corroborate abuse, then Chandler is up.' She paused, her eyes fixed on Brackman. 'And Tommy's no longer on the case.'

All heads, except Mullaney's, turned towards her; when she didn't elaborate, Brackman nodded grimly and said, 'Well, well. That should enhance our image.'

McKenzie, looking surprised and irritated by this news, but knowing there was nothing he could do about it, said impatiently, 'Just move along, Douglas. We don't have all day.'

'Right. Jonathan?' – Brackman's eyes had moved on to the young black attorney – 'In *re James Riley* . . .?'

'Yes, Douglas. James Riley.' Jonathan Rollins cleared his throat and began to read from his file: 'Captain Riley was shot down over North Vietnam in 1970. He was officially listed as missing-in-action. Three months ago, his wife died and left her entire estate to her husband.'

C.J. Lamb – the firm's resident English Rose, cool, power-dressed and gorgeous – looked at Rollins with eyebrows raised. 'She believed he's still alive?'

Beside her, Castroverti sat shaking his head. 'And still a POW? Aw come on – it's been over twenty years.'

Brackman said, 'Amazing how anyone can still believe those poor men are ever coming home.'

'How can you say that?' Ann Kelsey cried. 'What about all those sightings since the war?'

Rollins cut in smartly. 'Anyway, fact is Riley's younger son, Mike, is petitioning to have his father declared dead and the estate divided. Our client – his elder brother, Sean Riley – is fighting it. He wants to use the money to find his father.'

'Guy must be crazy!' Castroverti muttered loudly.

'Any chance of a settlement?' said Brackman.

'I've tried,' Rollins said. 'Trouble is, the brothers are barely speaking.'

'So it looks like a fight over a dead man?'

Rollins nodded. 'Only one party doesn't want to believe he's dead.'

'Okay,' said Brackman. 'Do what you can, Jonathan. Next item' – and he glowered slowly round the table – 'I understand there are questions about office assignments?'

'Just one, Douglas.' Stuart Markowitz had sat up eagerly, waiting for this moment. 'How come Susan Bloom got Mike Kuzak's office, when it wasn't offered to any of the Partners?'

'You could have put in for it, Stuart – but you didn't,' Brackman said briskly. 'And for the kind of rent she's paying, we can't very well give her *your* office.'

'Of course not,' Markowitz said, humbled.

'I'm glad you understand.' Brackman turned dismissively to the table. 'We're adjourned.'

As they stood up and began collecting their papers, Leland McKenzie moved across to where Mullaney was standing, just out of earshot of Grace. 'Tommy, can I see you for a moment?'

*

'I'd like you to reconsider.'

Tommy yawned and scratched his ear. 'She'll never beat the odds, Leland. And we both know it.'

'The jury could nullify. They could come in Not Guilty . . .'

'Sure. But when have you seen it happen? In the real world a "burning-bed" defence has to include insanity. If Elsa Chandler was in her right mind, they won't acquit.'

'You don't know that for sure,' Leland said. 'Grace is damned good. Don't underestimate her, Tommy.'

'Oh I don't, Leland! She's the best. But she just lost her baby – her marriage broke up – ' Tommy let the words hang; then after a moment added, 'Do *you* agree with her?'

'No,' Leland paused. 'But it's a legitimate defence and it's her case. Remember, she's an independent now – I can't dictate strategy to her. If she wants to take this risk, I can't stop her.'

Tommy shook his head. 'Everything I know says it's wrong. I don't know if I can back her.'

'It's up to you, of course. I'm not going to force you.' Leland's voice was gentle but firm. 'All I'm going to tell you is this, Tommy – right now, more than a Second Chair, Grace probably needs a friend.'

*

Chapter Five

Later that day, while the body and soul of Elsa Chandler were, quite literally, being fought over in L.A.'s Criminal Court, Leland McKenzie was back at his desk, quietly working through some documents from the firm's bank.

He was just reaching for the intercom, intending to call for some coffee and his favourite Italian biscuits, when the door burst open. There had been no knock, no warning. Susan Bloom strode in.

'Leland McKenzie – you're a stubborn old fart!'

The Senior Partner's whole body jerked back in his chair as though he'd received a powerful blow to the chest. 'Of all the . . .!' he began. '*Get out of here . . .!*'

But she swept in, not giving him time to finish. 'Don't splutter at me! – this is too important. We can do each other a lotta good.'

'I'd rather take a swim in nuclear waste!' Leland muttered, puce with anger.

'Get over it, honey. You can't afford pride – and nor can your firm.' She came over and sat down on the desk directly in front of him, invading his space with a dense, invisible cloud of scent that could have gassed a badger.

She was dressed today in a black satin trouser-suit spattered with luminous sequins, and her hair was scraped back like a shiny black bathing cap, except for a fringe of curly black ringlets across her brow. She looked like Lady Macbeth out of some vaudeville nightmare. Leland sat gaping up at her as she went on:

'This place is in deep doody and everybody knows it.' She avoided his horrified gaze. 'Just listen to my proposal. If you don't like it, *then* you can throw me out!'

'You have just two minutes,' Leland said, his voice like a drowning man's.

'I only need one,' Susan Bloom said. 'I'm a cash-cow – I've got more money than God. I'll pay whatever you want for office space and refer you all my litigation overflow, plus anything my clients need outside the industry. I'll even get you a deal with my insurance company.' She paused to get a cigarette in her mouth and lit it with a slim gold lighter in a seamless movement which would have left Bogart groping.

'In return for what?' he said, in a croak.

'Your downtown connections. Your sterling reputation. You need a shot in the arm, buddy-boy! And I want to branch out – *expand, diversify* . . . Together, we're like Fred Astaire and Ginger Rogers.' She gave a sudden, horrible giggle. 'She had the sex – he had the class . . .!'

Leland found he could not even swallow. He went on staring at her, like a rabbit before a snake. *Oh my God*, he thought, *this isn't happening. It just can't be happening! Please God – please Douglas! Wake me up . . .!*

Susan Bloom sat swinging one gross black-sequined leg from the desk, staring down at the tired grey face below her, drawing on her cigarette and giving him a coquettish grin.

42

Somehow, at last, he managed to speak. 'If you want a merger, it's out of the question.'

'I like to co-habit before I get married. We share space and see what happens.'

'Trust me – nothing will.'

'But you like my offer?' Susan gave a hard-boiled, flirtatious leer.

Leland braced himself and somehow managed to get into legal gear. He said, 'We'd have the right to terminate – at any time – at a month's notice. You pay for office services and use of the library. And joint clients are fifty-fifty.'

'My name goes on the door,' Bloom said, blowing smoke in his direction. 'We put out a press release and agree to talk closer ties in six months . . .'

'A year,' said Leland, waving the smoke out of his eyes. 'And this will have to be approved by the Partners. It isn't final . . .'

'Small strokes, baby! Paperwork.' And this time she gave him a wide enamelled smile that made him flinch. 'We've got a deal!'

Oh God, thought Leland again. *Just wake me up! Tell me this isn't real . . .*

*

The main Probate Court, in the County of Los Angeles, assembled next day at 10.30 a.m. The smog was as bad as ever and the small courtroom was both uncomfortable and oppressive.

The petitioner's counsel, Jane Maxon – a pretty young attorney in a white blouse and shapely grey skirt, like the head girl of a Swiss finishing-school – had called her client on to the stand. Mike Riley – younger son of the presumed-dead pilot, Captain James Riley, late of the U.S. Air Force – was a gaunt, sallow young man who had sat following the proceedings so far with a peculiar, shifting expression, by turns predatory and bored.

His older brother, Sean – sitting at the respondent's table next to his counsel, Jonathan Rollins – was his almost direct opposite: a well-built, open-faced man with the clear, unswerving gaze of an idealist. Observing the two of them together, Jonathan Rollins was in no doubt as to which of them Riley Snr. would be more proud to see today in court. He only hoped that old Judge Myron Swaybill, now presiding, would pick up some of those paternal vibes.

Mike Riley gave his evidence in a mechanical tone, without notes, as though he were used to reciting it many times to many people. He kept his flickering eyes on his attractive young attorney; not once did he even glance at his brother.

'My father was a pilot assigned to the 388th Tactical Fighter Wing. On May Second 1970 he was shot down over Hoa Binh Province. He radioed the plane was on fire and he was going to eject.'

'Was he heard from again?' Jane Maxon asked.

'No. By the time Search-and-Rescue reached the area, there was no sign of him. The plane had exploded on impact.'

'And at that time the Air Force classified him as Missing-in-Action?'

'Yes. But in '74 Mom was notified that his classification had been changed to K.I.A. – "Killed-in-Action".'

Jane Maxon nodded. 'And do you agree with that conclusion, Mr Riley?'

'I've read the file over and over – I've read it maybe a thousand times – just trying to find something' – his voice took on a tone of plaintive resentment – '*anything* that would let me believe he was still alive. But he isn't. My father's gone. He died in that crash.'

'Thank you, Mr Riley.' Jane Maxon sat down.

Jonathan Rollins took her place. His serious, boyish good looks and pleasant, persuasive manner always went down in court. Here, surely, was the American Dream come true: a living witness to multicultural progress, mused Judge Myron Swaybill, for even the most red-necked bigot from the boondocks, or crazed fanatic in the black ghettos, would have trouble objecting to a boy like Rollins . . . *A credit to the American legal system.* The judge decided to listen to him with special favour.

'You have no memory of your father, have you, Mr Riley?' Rollins began, in his soft mellifluous voice.

'Objection,' Jane Maxon broke in. 'Relevance?'

'His perception of his father's loss is directly relevant, Your Honour,' said Rollins.

'I'll allow it,' said Swaybill.

'I was only two when he was shot down,' Mike Riley answered. 'I remember a man who swung me over his head once. That's all.'

'In 1973,' Rollins went on, 'when a total of 591 POWs were returned to this country in "Operation Homecoming" – you were five years old? Do you remember that day? Watching it on T.V.?'

'Yes.'

'Do you remember what your mother did during the broadcast? As each man got off the plane and was reunited with his family?'

The young man's gaze shifted awkwardly round the courtroom, again without seeming to notice his older brother, sitting only a few feet away. 'She kept calling my Dad's name over and over,' he said at last. 'Kept saying, "*Jim . . . Please Jimmy . . . Come on, Jim . . .!*" He paused. 'She knew he wasn't on any of the lists. But she couldn't help it.'

'And when he wasn't one of the men who got off that plane, she started to cry. Then what did you do, Mr Riley?'

Mike Riley hesitated, obviously unhappy about answering.

'What did you do?' Rollins repeated.

'I . . . I took a picture of my dad and smashed it against the wall. I was five years old, Mr Rollins. I blamed my father for making her cry. But I grew out of that . . .'

'But over the years there were other family disagreements?'

'She and Sean couldn't stop hoping.'

'But they did have information that justified hope . . .'

Mike Riley leaned forward, showing the first signs of anger. 'The United States Government reviewed my father's case and determined he was dead!'

Rollins nodded. 'Yes – as part of a blanket ruling. A ruling that resulted in *all* M.I.A.s being declared dead.'

Jane Maxon cut in: 'Your Honour, is there a question here?'

'All twenty-three hundred of them,' said Rollins sharply.

'Mr Rollins, get to the point, please,' said the judge.

'Mr Riley, you stand to benefit from this proceeding, don't you?'

'What d'you mean?' For a moment Mike Riley was thrown.

'You're about to be married,' Rollins said. 'Maybe have a family. Inheriting three hundred and fifty thousand dollars – that's not a bad start.'

Mike Riley's mouth sank down at the edges, his lips bloodless with rage. 'Don't tell me about bad starts, Mr Rollins! I grew up watching my mother wasting her life – *waiting for the phone to ring . . .*'

*

On the stand was a solid, greying man in his fifties: straight-backed, clear-eyed, you could see he was a soldier from fifty paces, before he'd even started to speak. He wore a button-down Brooks Bros. shirt and dark lounge suit. Colonel Stephen Kellogg, on secondment to Washington as a Pentagon spokesman, was now in the L.A. Probate Court to give expert testimony in the case of Mike Riley, in the latter's attempt to get his father declared dead and buried – or burned, pulverised, torn apart by carrion crows, gnawed by tigers, chewed to nothing by ants and rodents – and so provide young Riley Jnr. with a comfortable *ex gratia* dowry with which to start married life.

Jane Maxon faced her witness with a certain flirtatious solemnity: attractive young woman with the older, more experienced man – neither of them forgetting for a moment, of course, that they were both professionals.

Col. Kellogg was saying: 'Yes – it is true that a blanket of death was imposed. However, the Department of Defence continues to operate under the assumption that some of those men might have survived.'

'What exactly is the Government doing, Colonel?'

'Our Defence Intelligence Agency has a special team

deployed in South-East Asia. Every lead about missing Americans is pursued and tracked down.'

'And yet not one soldier has emerged as a result of all this effort. Are you sure you're not just chasing rainbows, Colonel?'

Kellogg lowered his head a little, gave Jane Maxon a slow-burning stare, and finally said, 'Maybe we are. But even if only one – *one* U.S. Serviceman – is still alive, we owe it to him to get him out.'

'Colonel, in your expert opinion, is there any evidence to warrant continued hope on the part of this family?'

Col. Kellogg paused for a moment, then looked solemnly down at Jane Maxon and said, 'I hate giving up on any man, but in this case I see no evidence to support a claim that Captain Riley is still alive.'

'Thank you, Colonel.'

*

The military man looked down at Jonathan Rollins, summed him up at once as a nice, well-turned-out, intelligent-looking boy – the sort of young black the Army likes to train up as a responsible member of the U.S. Armed Forces. A straight arrow, Col. Kellogg decided.

'Colonel,' Rollins began, 'it's a matter of record that over the last eighteen years your agency has received a total of 11,933 reports concerning Americans in Indo–China – some as recent as the last few weeks. Correct?'

'Yes, that is so.'

'And of those 11,933 reports, Colonel, how many have been worthy of further investigation by your agency?'

'Approximately one hundred are still under investigation,' Col. Kellogg replied, po-faced.

'So out of over eleven thousand reports, any one of which might lead to the rescue of –' Rollins made a vague, graceful gesture – 'of these two men's father, you've determined that only one hundred – *a fraction of one per cent* – are worthy of further action?'

Col. Kellogg shrugged. 'You know how many con artists are out there, peddling false hope to M.I.A. families, Counsellor? Faking sightings for money – bogus photos – alleged eye-witness reports . . .? Most of this information is no better than rumour, and some of it a lot less.'

Rollins reached for a document off the respondent's table. 'Colonel, is it true that in 1985 – after repeated petitionings from Mrs Riley – you finally permitted her to see a partially declassified report of one of these "rumours" which related to her husband's capture?'

Kellogg frowned. He found himself liking this young black attorney rather less now. 'It did not relate to her husband. The reported incident pertained to the capture of another pilot, John Harwood, whose remains have already been repatriated.'

'But Major Harwood was flying an F-4 Phantom, was he not? And the witness clearly stated he saw a pilot parachute from an F-105 – the plane James Riley was flying?'

The Colonel stared down at Rollins. 'The date indicated Harwood,' he said blankly.

'But the location of the observer was in fact closer to Captain Riley's position than Major Harwood's.'

The Colonel began showing signs of being worried. 'The testimony was riddled with inconsistencies.'

'And in the face of those inconsistencies,' Rollins went on, 'isn't it your agency's policy to dismiss these sightings?'

'Absolutely not!'

Rollins leant forward, his voice low and confident. 'Opening cases is "counter-productive" – isn't it, Colonel? You're more interested in closing them . . .?'

Suddenly Kellogg was furious: with the spontaneous, resentful fury of the senior man challenged by one much younger, and a civilian, too – but also with the defensive fury of the Government placeman jealously holding the official line against an impertinent intruder. He now stood leaning slightly forward, head lowered, both hands on the rail. He spoke slowly, with perfect control:

'There were seventy-eight thousand M.I.A.s in World War Two – eight thousand in Korea. Not a *single one* of those men ever came back. We have a responsibility to the M.I.A.s – yes. But we also have a responsibility to their families. And we're not about to mislead them – to encourage them to wait for men who are *not* coming home!'

'And despite the evidence in your own files, you still insist that Captain James Riley is not one of those men?'

'The so-called "evidence" is not – in our judgment – enough to support the belief that he's still alive.'

Rollins nodded. 'Short of Captain Riley handing you the file himself, Colonel, I wonder what *would* make you believe it.'

Chapter Six

Meanwhile, over at the Criminal Court, the atmosphere was very different. Menace was in the air. A heavy, dignified, well-disciplined menace. For this was no theoretical debate over possibilities – a balancing of the odds, long past, on whether a certain man, left over from a long and ghastly war, might still be alive or not. Here, in the Criminal Court, in the County of Los Angeles, Death was all around: etched in every legal face, concealed in every briefcase, its bony finger-marks on every official document.

Death stalked the benches of the court, hovered on the shoulders of counsel, incited the packed benches of the Press, stood patiently behind the old buzzard-head of Judge Walter Green. Above all, it hung heavy and dark round the bowed neck of Elsa Chandler.

Its presence also haunted the woman's only defender, the lovely, tragic Grace Van Owen. This morning, Grace had called her latest witness to the stand: a leggy, dizzy-looking blonde called Layne Novak, dressed in the very latest-but-one *dernier cri* from Paris via a reach-me-down discount store on Belmont. The girl was resting her shapely body against the rail of the stand, as though she'd strained her back on the casting-couch.

'Ms Novak, what was your relationship with the late Ralph Chandler?' Grace Van Owen asked her.

'We slept together. For a while.' She made it sound like a few games of tennis at the country club.

'During his marriage?'

'Sure. From 1986 to 1988.'

Grace turned to the judge. 'Your Honour, both parties stipulate that Ralph Chandler's engagement calendars for those years show regular appointments with this witness several times a week.' She turned back to her witness: 'Ms Novak, during these times, did Mr Chandler ever exhibit abusive behaviour towards you?'

'Yeah, well – at first it was just verbal. Y'know?'

'I don't know, Ms Novak. Tell me.'

'Well – he liked to kinda *insult* me. It used to arouse him. Then it got heavier. One day he went too far. He started to slap me around. Things got pretty ugly.'

'What happened, exactly?'

'Well – let's just say it got so it wasn't a *game* any more. He knocked me out cold. When I came to, I was a mess.' Layne Novak raised a hand and began examining her ox-blood nails. 'Both my eyes were swollen shut. I was bruised all over and my shoulder was dislocated.'

'Did you see Ralph Chandler after that?'

'He tried to force me. He just wouldn't back off. I got so scared I moved and changed my phone to an unlisted number.'

'Thank you, Ms Novak.'

Deputy Assistant Attorney Graphia unfolded his sleek body from the chair. 'Ms Novak' – his voice was all honey over steel – 'did you accept money from Mr Chandler?'

'Objection!' said Grace. 'Relevance.'

Graphia snapped back, 'Goes to the witness's credibility.'

'Overruled,' said Judge Green.

Graphia turned back to the girl. 'Did you accept money from Ralph Chandler?' he said again.

'I'm not a call girl!' she cried, genuinely outraged.

'But you let Mr Chandler pay your rent for a year,' Graphia said, his lips parted in a half-smile. 'He bought you expensive clothes and jewellery . . .'

'That didn't give him the right to use me as a punching-bag!' the girl replied, not unreasonably.

Graphia nodded. 'In fact, there's no proof Ralph Chandler did anything to you. Is there? You never sought treatment for your injuries. You never told anyone. We only have *your* word that Chandler beat you.'

'It's the truth!'

'Is it?' Graphia's black eyebrows lifted a good inch. 'Or did you agree to testify so that you could sell the film rights of your story . . .?'

Grace was on her feet. '*Objection!* That's totally without foundation!'

'No it isn't,' Graphia sliced back like a dagger. He looked slowly round the court, his eyes hooded with certain triumph. 'Last week Ms Novak here signed a contract with "Creative Talent International", for film and television representation.'

There was a stir round the courtroom. Grace looked aghast, while beside her Tommy Mullaney sank down several inches in his seat, drawing a hand over his mouth and jaw. 'She never said a word!' he muttered.

Layne Novak stared desperately at Graphia and said, in a half-gulp, 'I'm an actress . . .'

'Oh, I agree,' – Graphia was smiling openly now – 'and you're putting on quite a performance right now. But it is not your profession . . .'

'Objection,' said Grace. 'This whole line of questioning is irrelevant.'

'It establishes the witness as a publicity-seeker with a profit motive, Your Honour,' said Graphia.

'I'll allow it,' said Judge Green.

'I repeat,' said Graphia. 'Are you trying to sell the story of your relationship with Ralph Chandler to Hollywood?'

The girl's vivid mouth went slack, her shoulders slumped. 'Yes,' she said at last, very quietly.

'No more questions,' said Graphia.

Grace and Tommy looked at each other, and found no comfort in what they saw. Graphia had won the round, and there was nothing they could do. Tommy let out his breath in a long hiss. *Bitch*, he breathed into the palm of his hand.

*

While Layne Novak was trashing what chances Elsa Chandler still had of ever breathing God's free air again, Arnie Becker, the City's combined middle-aged heart-throb and ace-divider of spoils in the divorce-game, was browsing through the dreary deposition of some rich, resentful matron from Desert Hot Springs who'd decided her husband weighed too much in bed and so was claiming she needed a separation 'in order to re-examine the parameters of her material relationship, and perhaps travel a little . . .'

Outside the smog was at last lifting. Arnie had his shoes off, his stockinged feet up on the table, and every few seconds the draught from the desk fan brushed luxuriously against his cheek. There was a tap on the open door. A large face with bright eyes and a lot of carefully applied make-up was beaming round at him.

'Hi! We haven't met yet. I'm Susan Bloom.'

Arnie stared at her, then lowered his feet and began to struggle up. 'Uh – hi. I'm Arnie Becker.' He paused. 'You're . . . You're not quite what I expected.'

'Yeah, I left my fangs and death-ray at home.' She shrugged. 'I know – they make a lousy first impression!' She came in and settled herself in the client's chair in front of him. She was dressed today in a sober blue skirt and tartan blouse with some rather fetching, frothy lace at the neck. Pity about the hips and ankles, Becker thought. Her face wasn't altogether bad-looking.

'Nice office,' she said, looking round. 'Your Senior Partner oughtta take a hint.'

'What – Leland?'

'Yeah. He's just mad with me! Somebody reported back to him that I said his room was *tacky*.' She gave a little giggle. 'Well, what else could I say? Your old McKenzie hardly works out of Michael Jackson's boudoir!' She swung her leg in front of him, looking round again and smiling with approval. 'But this is *nice*, Arnie!'

'Thanks. I've redecorated.'

'Yeah – I hear you're hell on lava-lamps! Mind if I smoke?'

'Well, actually . . .' he began, and watched helplessly as she got out a cigarette and lit it before he could properly register his protest.

'Thanks.' She inhaled deeply. 'Something's come up, Arnie, that I think you might be interested in. You know Steve Graham?'

'Local reporter with Channel Three?'

'Right. He's going on vacation and the Station's looking for someone to sub for him for a couple of weeks. The exec-producer's a client of mine. I told him I'd look around.'

Becker was sitting rather awkwardly. 'Well, I'm flattered, but . . . Hell, Susan – I'm no journalist!'

'Don't have to be,' Susan Bloom said, sending a quick jet of smoke barrelling up to the ceiling. 'They've got reporters to do all the research, and writers to write the copy. All you have to do is read it. Plus, once a week, you take phone calls – just a little improvised legal advice.' She paused, breathing twin exhaust fumes out of both nostrils.

He looked at her blankly. 'But I'm a divorce lawyer,' he said at last.

'You went to Law School, didn't you? You know the difference between a crime and a tort?'

'This is only temporary – right?'

Susan Bloom looked deliberately vague. 'That's what they say. But my hunch is, they're looking to dump Stevie-Boy – past his TV shelf-life, you know. But I could be wrong.' She stood up and pressed out her half-smoked cigarette in his big copper ornamental tray. 'Sleep on it, baby – and get back to me tomorrow morning. They're looking to jump on this by week's end. Nice to meet you, Arnie!'

She was starting to leave, when Becker remembered: 'What's in this for you?'

She shrugged a big shoulder. 'Favour to a client.'

'Yeah, but why me?' What are *my* qualifications?'

Susan Bloom turned, giving the full Cleopatra look. '*You kidding?* Women between eighteen and thirty-four are just gonna *lose* themselves in those big blue eyes . . .!'

For some moments after she'd gone he just stared at the door. *Why stop at thirty-four?* he thought. Arnie Becker, TV Presenter . . . Arnie Becker, the Coast's new heart-throb. The Legal Eagle with all the answers to every problem, every prayer . . . He tried it out several times, and each time the more he liked it.

*

'With self-defence alone, there's no compromise for the jury.' Grace was walking slowly, purposefully, back and forth in front of the table in her office. Below her, Elsa Chandler sat stiff and nervous, like a cornered deer. Tommy Mullaney was half-sprawled beside her, listening.

'They have to acquit,' she went on, 'or find you guilty. There's no middle way. And if they find you guilty, you get the death penalty.'

'If we give them a fallback,' Tommy said, 'not guilty by reason of insanity – they'll probably take it.' His slow, grey eyes moved over Elsa Chandler's distraught face. 'You won't go to prison, Elsa, but the judge will have to commit you.'

'To a mental hospital,' she said, in a cold, dead voice. She shuddered. 'I couldn't stand that.'

'Chances are,' said Tommy, 'it wouldn't be for long. But there are no guarantees.'

Elsa Chandler stared bleakly back at him. And it occurred to Tommy that if one of the heroines of Greek tragedy had worn make-up and used an expensive hair-dresser, she'd look like this.

'Ralph used to tell me I was crazy,' she said at last. 'That I needed him because I was mentally unstable – emotionally disturbed. For a long time,' – she sniffed and pulled out a handkerchief – 'for a long time I believed it.' She looked up at Tommy, then at Grace, and a small, brave attempt at defiance came into her voice. 'I'll never believe it again. *Never!*' She stuffed the handkerchief into her sleeve and sat up straight.

'I want to go for self-defence.'

*

Chapter Seven

T.V.'s new 'face'-to-be, the coast's future Agony 'Uncle' Extraordinary relaxed under the cool sheet, in a quiet little hotel room on the road out to Pacific Palissades.

With the smog at last gone, the bright ocean sun peeped through the drawn blinds. Next to him, nestling comfortably under his arm, was the buxom shape of Ms Roxanne Melman. Her rich dark hair lay slightly tousled against the pillow; her eyes were half-closed, the sheet pulled up demurely over her full breasts; while Arnold Becker brushed his lips lightly across her upper arm, planting little kisses like a row of invisible petals on the downy skin.

'Is it past lunchtime?' she said sleepily.

'Still hungry?'

'Douglas is going to be wondering where I am?' She shifted her position, snuggling closer to him.

'Tell him you stopped by the Hyatt for something quick and easy.'

'Like me? – quick and easy . . .!' – she squeezed his arm, with a little sex-kitten giggle: – '*Ah honey, jus' come up to my room some afternoon and let's have a lovely, quick, easy one-afternoon stand. . . .*' She spoke in a low, langorous, slightly husky voice – the seductive, bedroom voice of every movie-siren since Becker's boyhood. She had not tried it on him before and he found it wildly sexy.

'Not that we have to do this,' he said. 'We both have perfectly good beds.'

'Oh but I like it!' she mewed, lifting her legs into the foetal position and burrowing her head under the crook of his arm.

It was irresistible. He hurled himself across her, and she gave a happy squeal and fought him playfully off.

'I have to get back to the office,' she said, some time later, in her natural voice. 'We both do.' She kissed him hard on the mouth, then sprang up, half-draped with the bedsheet, and began to dress quickly. Becker sat up, yawned, and began to follow her, more slowly. Neither of them was keen to leave.

'So what are you gong to tell Susan Bloom?' she said at last, smoothing her skirt down.

'Oh God, I don't know.' Becker stretched wearily and pulled on his boxer shorts. 'Hell, Rox, I don't *want* to be a celebrity! I tell you – when I did the video, I wound up getting kidnapped at gunpoint. I mean,' he added, putting on his shirt, 'who needs the *tsursis*?'

'There is that,' Roxanne agreed, wriggling her toes into her shoes.

'And it's probably not the image the firm wants to project. I mean, being on the news, that's one thing. But a phone-in lawyer . . .?'

She stood patting her hair in front of the mirror. 'Leland would probably think it "undignified",' she said.

'Yeah – and Douglas . . . He'd go take a high kick at the moon! High profiles attract high-profile cases – just the

60

kinda thing Douglas hates most. If I took the job, he'd have my baby!'

'Huh-huh.' She paused to do a last skimming repair-job on her eyeshadow.

'And the *people* in the industry, Rox! Power-junkies, all of them. Narcissists! People who can't walk down the sidewalk without expecting a round of applause. What the hell do I have in common with people like that?'

'I can't imagine,' Roxanne said, turning and smoothing down her hips again. She was ready now.

Arnie had put on his trousers, and reached for his jacket. 'I just don't think I'm cut out for it. I'm too *sensitive*! They eat guys like me for breakfast.'

Roxanne had picked up her handbag. 'Right, Arnie . . . Speaking of eating, you want to grab a fast sandwich in the coffee shop?'

'Yeah, sure. Let's stop at the news-stand too. I think they carry *Variety*.'

Roxanne was smiling to herself as they went out. *Poor old Arnie!* Whatever he might say in self-defence, he was half-hooked already. She, on the other hand, was completely hooked – on *him* – and she loved it. She'd always secretly wanted to make home-base with the gorgeous Arnie Becker. Now she'd not only made it – she was ready for the next pitch.

*

Tim Bryerley was a powerfully-built man, with the thick-ened features and shrewd eyes of a retired footballer who can think on his feet.

He answered Jonathan Rollins in a clear, methodical

voice: 'I served three tours of duty in Saigon with Army Intelligence. I monitored and analysed enemy radio transmissions. Basically eavesdropping.'

'In that capacity, did you have access to information about P.O.W.s?'

'I did. Our equipment was very sophisticated. If the V.C. radioed they had a prisoner, we'd pick right up on it. We were able to track hundreds of our men that way.'

'Would a prisoner like James Riley have had value to the North Vietnamese?' Rollins asked.

'Absolutely. They wanted live prisoners. Especially guys with technical training – like pilots.'

'And after our troops pulled out in 1973, what did they do then?'

'Most of my civilian work in Saigon is still classified,' Bryerley said. 'But I served off and on until 1975 as a translator to the American team that was discussing the return of the M.I.As with the North Vietnamese.'

Rollins leaned forward, his black eyes alert. 'There were meetings that took place *after* President Nixon announced that all P.O.W.s had been returned? Right?'

'Right.' Brierley shrugged. 'It was no secret. It was part of the Paris Agreement.'

'Then it's your expert opinion that there were American P.O.W.s held in Vietnam after the 1973 release?'

'Like I said, I tracked several hundred P.O.W.s during the war. They were alive when I left. Not a single one of those men came home.'

In silence, Rollins sat down. Jane Maxon took his place. 'But Captain Riley wasn't among those men you tracked?' she asked, in a deceptively off-hand voice.

'No,' said Bryerley.

'In fact, in spite of your sophisticated technology, you have no knowledge that Captain Riley even *survived* the crash?'

The witness hesitated a second. 'No.'

'Mr Bryerley,' – Jane Maxon's voice was like cold silk – 'you were asked to resign from your civilian position with Army Intelligence? Isn't that correct?'

'We had a difference of opinion,' Bryerley said stiffly.

'Were you asked to resign? Yes or No?'

Bryerley began to garble his words: 'Our Government knew there were . . . that there were men . . .'

'*Yes or No!*' Jane Maxon repeated.

'. . . There were men left behind out there! I was told to shut up and stay out of it!'

'Answer the question, Mr Bryerley,' said Judge Swaybill.

Mike Bryerley stood, gritting his teeth. 'Yes,' he said at last. 'I was asked to resign.'

'In fact, for inadequate job performance.'

'That's a load of crap!' he said savagely.

'Is it, Mr Bryerley? Since 1975 you've lost four other positions for poor work performance – poor attitude – absenteeism . . .'

'Why don't we talk about the jobs I held successfully?' Bryerley's face was taut and white; a nerve was beginning to tug furiously at the corner of his mouth.

'Why don't we?' Jane Maxon said, almost gleefully. 'For the last eight years, most of your income has derived from your status as an "expert" on P.O.W.s – hasn't it? If this issue disappeared, so would your livelihood.'

'That isn't true.'

'But you did earn over 35,000 dollars this year alone, from speaking engagements and magazine articles?'

Bryerley scowled and gave a little shrug. 'I don't make that much every year . . .' he muttered.

'So this was a good year in the M.I.A. business?' Jane Maxon said waspishly; then, without a pause, 'I have no further questions, your Honour.'

*

The same morning a surprise Press Conference was held in the reception lobby of McKenzie Brackman & Partners. Susan Bloom, in a purple tent of a dress topped with pink ribbons the size of soup tureens, held the floor. Next to her stood her latest client: a massive, misshapen young man who looked at first as though he was being supported by two Olympic athletes, each crouching to take the weight of his legs – until you realised they *were* his legs. This creature was 'Beef' Barstow, the big up-and-coming name on the Californian wrestling circuit.

Susan Bloom was singing his praises to the assembled reporters and T.V. crews, in a voice that could have addressed Shea Stadium without a loudspeaker:

'In professional wrestling today,' she boomed, 'there's nobody bigger than Beef Barstow! He's a star of the first magnitude and an inspiration to millions of kids all over the West Coast. I take great pleasure in announcing my representation of him – *and* of his new company, "All Beef Productions", which is already negotiating major film and T.V. projects . . .'

The reporters' voices cracked in like whips: '*Does that mean Beef's giving up wrestling . . .?*' '*Beef, you really think you can make it in pictures . . .?*' '*What about your tax problems, Beef . . .?*'

Susan Bloom held up both arms, like an outsize goddess outside her temple calling upon the unruly multitude. 'Give him a break guys! One at a time – *please!*'

A reporter snapped back: *'Beef, is it true your wife is going to sue you for back-alimony . . .?'*

Barstow gave a growl, like a beast at bay: 'Daria's still in love with me!'

'So how come she's taking you to court?'

'Back off, man,' the big man snarled, curling his great hands at his sides and taking a step forward; but Bloom, smiling like a lighthouse, grabbed his arm. 'We'd like someone else to have a chance. You – the corner!'

A woman reporter shrilled: *'Does Beef see himself as a leading man?'*

Another, nearer the front: *'C'mon Beef! Stop hiding behind your lawyer! Your fans have a right to know.'*

'Wait your turn, please!' Bloom bawled.

'Did you stiff your wife and Uncle Sam?' the first reporter asked aggressively.

Beef Barstow's huge, ugly body lunged forward. 'I said back off, Jack!' he roared.

Just then, behind them all, the lift doors opened and Leland McKenzie and the trim figure of C.J. Lamb appeared in the reception area. They both stopped dead, staring at the media circus in front of them. 'What in the world?' Leland gasped.

C.J. could scarcely help herself bursting out laughing at the fearful spectacle that now unfolded on the very threshold of McKenzie Brackman's august premises, and all in the full glare of T.V.

Seeing what was coming, Susan Bloom had hurled her impressive weight on to her client's arm, in a vain effort to restrain him from reaching the offending newsman, who had skipped tactically behind the ranks of the other reporters. But he was not fast enough – or his colleagues failed to provide the cover he needed.

The great brute, moving with astonishing speed, shook his arm free of Bloom and burrowed into the crowd of newsmen, scattering them like nine-pins. In a flash – upsetting a huge indoor plant – he cornered his victim, and with an ugly howl, head-butted him into a heap on the marble floor. Susan Bloom came billowing across, like a galleon in full-sail, yelling; while the reporters scrambled around, trying – without much success – to drag the snorting 'Beef' Barstow away from the crumpled shape at his feet.

The reporter lay huddled up, trying to protect his head with his arms, and for one exciting moment, it looked as though the cameras might be treated to an even more awe-inspiring spectacle: a wrestling bout between 'Beef' Barstow and the great Susan Bloom, who was now struggling manfully to save him from a battery charge, or worse.

The TV crew was ecstatic, the cameras moving in hungrily to devour this true Battle of the Titans, with Bloom bellowing at the wrestler, as though he were a large dangerous dog off its leash: '*Beef* – get off! Leave him!'

'Flying drop-kick?' C.J. Lamb murmured, unable to suppress an impish grin. Leland McKenzie stood by, utterly aghast.

*

Pham Tuan was a slender, delicate-boned Vietnamese in a dark light-weight suit that would always be too loose for

66

him. He looked anything between twenty-five and fifty years old – a scholarly man, his face hollowed by the unmistakable marks of malnutrition and long privations in a labour camp. To these was added the parched, slightly paper complexion that invades the Annamite skin when exposed to too much smog and stress. His voice was quiet, pleasant, his English immaculate:

'There were four Americans at Quyet Tien,' he told the court. 'They were kept in their own place – away from the rest of us.'

'You were also a prisoner there, Mr Tuan?' Rollins asked him.

The Vietnamese man replied, with bitter dignity, 'It was one of the camps I was sent to for "re-education".'

'How did you know these four men were Americans?' Rollins asked.

'The guards called them "G.I. Number Ten" – Phan paused – 'it is an insulting term for Americans.'

'Could you describe the appearance of these men?'

'They were very thin. Their uniforms were torn and dirty.'

'And how were they treated?'

'Life in the camp is harsh, Mr Rollins. But for the Americans it is particularly cruel.' (Rollins noted the use of '*is*' – a nice touch, he thought.) 'Some mornings they were marched out into the yard,' Pham Tuan went on. 'The guards made them stand there many hours. No sitting. No shade. No talking.' The court had grown very quiet.

'Did you have any direct contact with any of these men, Mr Tuan?'

'Several times. I brought them water. One time, in the earth next to the tall one, I saw the letters R . . I . . L . . E . . . Y.

67

He had written them with his foot. Then a guard moved closer. When I looked down again, the letters were gone.

'When did this happen?' said Rollins. The court was as quiet as an empty church.

'Five years ago. April, 1986.'

Rollins picked up a black-and-white photograph and advanced to the stand, holding up for the witness to see. 'Was this the man you saw?'

Pham Tuan nodded. 'Yes.'

Suddenly the spell in the hushed courtroom was shattered. 'That's a lie!' Mike Riley yelled, his face white, distorted with anger.

'*Mr Riley – please!*' It was Judge Swaybill's turn to look angry.

On the stand Pham Tuan nodded again, unmoved. 'That is the man.'

Quivering with fury, Mike Riley was out of his chair now, waving a long forefinger towards the photograph which was now in the Vietnamese man's hand. 'That picture is twenty years old! How could you possibly tell . . .?'

His brother, Sean, called out from the respondent's table, 'Why can't you believe him?'

Judge Swaybill cut in, 'Both of you! *That's quite enough!*'

But Mike Riley was not to be restrained. Still on his feet, and shaking with rage, he shouted at the judge, 'Why don't you tell him he's under oath here?' – then rounded on Pham Tuan – 'You know what this means?'

'*Mr Riley!*' the judge roared.

The elder brother, Sean, looked at Pham Tuan, then at Swaybill. 'He's telling the truth,' he said gravely.

But Mike Riley was still on his feet. 'My mother sponsored his entire family!' he cried, jabbing a hand furiously at the Vietnamese man, who remained motionless, without expression. 'She paid for them to come over here! What do you *expect* him to say?'

Judge Swaybill had risen from his chair: 'I will not tolerate this! Counsellors, you have twenty minutes. Don't bring your clients back into my courtroom till they're under control!'

*

In the small witness room the tension crackled like electricity. Rollins had come in first; he turned to the others, determined on a damage-limitation exercise. 'Now please. Everyone! We'd like to make some peace here.' He paused, catching Sean Riley's eye, and the elder brother gave Rollins a quick nod.

'My client wants to propose a settlement,' Rollins said.

Jane Maxon interrupted: 'I don't know if the court would approve it. But let's hear it, anyway.'

'Fifty-thousand dollars,' Rollins said quietly.

Mike Riley gave a snorting noise, like an overheated horse. 'And the rest goes to guys like Pham?' he sneered. 'Forget it, Sean!'

Sean looked for a moment wonderingly, pityingly at his younger brother. 'How do you do it, Mike? How do you hear a story like that guy's and just not feel *anything?*'

'I gave up on the stories,' Mike Riley said bitterly, 'after the commando with the phony dog-tags. You let Mom get taken in by that nut . . .!'

'It was her decision,' Sean said, suddenly beginning to lose his cool. 'And her money . . .'

'Sure – and she felt like a fool afterwards.'

'Mike, he's your father too. This is about saving his life.' The elder brother was on the point of tears.

'Yeah – and how about saving *our* lives? We have to move on, Sean. We have to forget . . .'

'No!' said Sean. 'He was my father. Even if it takes the rest of my life, I'm going to find him.'

Mike Riley came closer and faced his older brother, their faces only a few inches apart. 'Then the judge had better declare us all dead! We died the day he crashed in the jungle.'

Jonathan Rollins and Jane Maxon stood by helplessly. Rollins felt slightly sickened.

*

At Morning Conference some of the firm were inclined to make light of the debacle in the reception-hall, which had led the local T.V. news on every bulletin that morning. It also headed the Conference agenda. 'In re yesterday's Press Conference,' Brackman began, with stupendous dignity and restraint, 'Susan Bloom has agreed to replace the glass door in Reception and to buy the firm a new Tunisian baby-palm.' He paused, glowering down the table as though to challenge anyone to smile, let alone laugh.

'She has also managed to persuade young Geraldo, of *The Sentinel*, not to file suit.'

'You're kidding?' said Markowitz.

'Best two falls out of three,' Becker said, grinning.

'This is not funny,' Leland McKenzie growled. He looked at Brackman. 'We just can't have the firm disrupted in this way, Douglas. It's frankly beyond endurance!'

70

'And I hate to bring it up,' Ann Kelsey broke in, 'but can we do something about her smoking in the hallways?'

'And monopolising the photocopying machine,' said Stuart.

'She must grind her coffee beans ten times a day,' Castroverti put in, his smile veiling his malice against Bloom.

'Oh come on, she's not that bad,' C.J. said. 'With Bloom around, at least the firm's not so . . .'

'Boring?' Stuart said, raising his eyebrows; he resented the implication because he knew C.J. was right.

Brackman had turned to Leland. 'We did make the six o'clock news last night, and most of this morning,' he said defensively.

'That kind of publicity,' the Senior Partner replied, 'is worse than none at all. Bloom was your idea, Douglas. Speak to her.'

Douglas Brackman knew it was useless to argue. Susan Bloom was his bag – and a mighty heavy one at that. Still, she was bringing in the dollars, as she'd promised – and if Leland didn't like the way she did it, well . . .

*

As it was, Brackman had more than just dear old Leland McKenzie to deal with, on the tricky subject of Susan Bloom. That evening he had a visit from an angry, articulate Roxanne. She'd caught him in his office just as he was packing his briefcase, ready to head home. He'd have felt better immured behind a stack of law papers, with telephones shrilling all round. This way he felt, wholly without justification, as though he were skiving. Foolishly, he attempted to fob her off, to bluff it out.

Roxanne stood there, arms akimbo, trying to look him defiantly in the eye. 'I'm telling you, Douglas – it's becoming a nightmare for everyone! Last week she commandeered five secretaries to get out a contract. She brought in enough Chinese food for sixty people, then left the trash all over the file room. Benny was almost in tears. So were the cleaning staff.'

Brackman said distractedly, as he rifled through the documents on the desk, before stuffing them into his case: 'Oh God . . . trust accountings, legal opinions . . .' His noble, forbidding head was secretly spinning: he'd never been quite able to stand up to Roxanne, and he was already scared stiff of his awesome protegée, Bloom.

Roxanne ploughed on, growing impatient with her boss's incipient weakness: 'She tips the building crew – and that makes everybody else here look cheap – and her cappuccino-maker leaked all over the bullpen rug . . .'

Brackman looked up and groaned: 'Stock certificates – offering circulars . . . *Oh God . . .!*'

'Douglas!' Roxanne said, in her most level, no-nonsense Mid-West tones. 'Somebody has to do something!'

Brackman straightened up suddenly and snapped the briefcase shut. If he were a less sanguine man, he'd have been sweating. Instead, he frowned. 'You're absolutely right. And *you're* going to do it!'

'Me?' Roxanne stared.

'You're the office manager, Rox. This is an office problem.'

'I'm not supposed to manage the lawyers,' she protested. 'You're the managing partner . . .'

'Exactly. And since we'd like to maintain friendly relations with Bloom, I should be the good cop. Which makes you the bad cop.'

'I don't make a good bad cop . . .'

'Because you're a woman?' Brackman said, glowering. 'I hope that's not what I'm hearing, Roxanne.' He picked up his briefcase and strode to the door. 'Stand your ground – don't let her bulldoze you. If you can handle Arnold Becker, you can handle Susan Bloom. Just lay down the law.'

She watched him go out. *You poor schmuck*, she thought.

Chapter Eight

There was tension in the small courtroom, but of a very different kind from the formal, insidious tension of the Criminal Court, where a woman's life was in the balance and the very air was contaminated with the faint subversive smell of the gas chamber.

Here, in the case of Riley versus Riley, in the L.A. Probate Court, it was the taste of bile, and the nasty, cat fight sounds of a bitter family quarrel in which filial loyalty was pitted against old childhood resentments, envy, and naked greed.

Jonathan Rollins and his adversary, Jane Maxon, had managed to reimpose a thin layer of restraint and good manners on their respective clients; and Judge Myron Swaybill had been persuaded, for the moment, to allow the proceedings to continue.

Jane Maxon rose to her feet. 'Madelyn Riley spent twenty years tenderly keeping a memory alive,' she began. 'We're all moved by the loyalty she felt for James Riley. She never stopped loving him. She never remarried, either. She never even considered it. Madelyn Riley gave up her life for her husband . . .' She paused, allowing the gravitas of her words to have their effect. The little court room remained very quiet.

'And now,' she said slowly, sadly, 'Sean Riley here is giving up *his* life, in the same empty pursuit – chasing the same dream that she did.' She leant forward slightly. '*Would James Riley have wanted this?* Or would he have wanted his family to get on with their lives?' She stepped back and stood shaking her head before going on:

'There is *no* credible evidence that James Riley is still alive. There's only the testimony of a Vietnamese refugee who owes his family's relocation to Madelyn Riley. It's not proof. It's a shred of hope which Sean Riley has convinced himself is a fact.' She paused again. Still not a sound, not a murmur in the courtroom. 'Mike Riley doesn't want to live off hope any more. He wants a normal life. Let him honour his father's memory – let him give James Riley a decent, proper burial.'

She turned slowly and sat down, in total silence. When Rollins took her place, he was all too aware that he was up against the odds, that the case could go either way. 'In 1969,' he began, 'the U.S. Government told Madelyn Riley that her husband was needed to stop Communism in Vietnam. And she believed them. In 1970, the Government told her that James Riley had been shot down, but that everything possible was being done to secure his release. *And again she believed them.* But in 1974, when the Government issued its blanket death-certificate for all M.I.A.s' – Rollins turned slightly to the court, letting his next words drop like stones into a well: – 'When that death certificate was issued, then Mrs Riley *stopped believing them.*'

He spread his pale brown hands in a gesture of mute

resignation. 'And *then* what did the Government do? It called peace demonstrators traitors, for undermining our troops in Vietnam. Then, in 1974, the same Government betrayed the troops who were left behind. And why? Because the M.I.A.s were so many loose ends, reminders of a war everyone wanted to forget. And in the seventeen long years since, the Government have done their best to forget. Done their best to ignore, to discredit or suppress any evidence that contradicts what they want to believe – and *what they want the rest of us to believe*. And I'll tell you why! Because if they admit there are M.I.A.s still alive today, they'd have to do something about it!'

There was real passion in Rollins' voice now, as his dark eyes passed over the sullen figure of Mike Riley, and on to that of his elder brother, straight and dignified, listening intently. Rollins went on to conclude:

'These are the facts. A witness near where Captain Riley was shot down saw a pilot parachute from the same plane as his. In 1986, a Vietnamese prisoner saw a fellow-prisoner – *an American* – write the name 'Riley' in the dirt, and later identified that American, here in this court, from a picture of James Riley. In *1986*! Your Honour, there *is* credible evidence that Captain Riley is still alive. The Government has abandoned him. Please! – don't force his family to do the same.'

He was done. There was nothing more he could say or do for Sean Riley, or for his father, dead or alive. The rest was up to Judge Myron Swaybill.

*

The T.V. studio was bright, hot, noisy, chaotic. The

moment the light came on for the commercial break, it was like the signal for a frenzied party to begin. A two-minute party, with all the gabbling, open-mouthed glitz and hyped-up mindlessness of which these ineffable celebs of the small screen were capable. Indeed, they knew nothing else. You either loved it all, or you kept away.

Arnie Becker had not kept away. He was right up there in the middle, secured like a tethered beast to a gigantic payroll. Under the excruciating glare of the lights, he sat smiling vacantly, while a thin varnish of make-up and anti-shine powder baked into a sticky mask over his handsome face. With him at the anchor desk was Julie Rayburn, a gorgeous, grinning creature with hair like spun gold, and eyes that looked as though they could open a cast-iron safe from thirty yards. There was a man with her – fellow-presenter Mike Rodriguez – who might have been her twin, with the same dayglo tan, horrible white teeth and great *bouffe* of hair, like a golden wig. (*Oh come back, Errol Flynn!* Becker thought secretly.) His face muscles were beginning to ache with the effort of maintaining his smile.

Across the floor below him, a man who looked as playful as a Pekingese who'd just won top prize in a dog show, come waltzing over the floor that was littered with coils of cable like the bottom of a snake pit. He was the director. Arnie Becker saw him and raised a hand, with the artificial *bonhomie* that was the password of the L.A. celeb-trail. He was learning fast. 'Hi Jake!'

'Hi Arnie. Okay?'

'Well – this earset's a little snug . . .'

'Sure, you can take it out when we go to tape. Everybody does.' Without realising it, they were both shouting, although they were barely a couple of feet away from each

77

other. 'Listen,' Jake added. 'Small change of plans,' he shouted, and dropped a sheaf of papers in front of Becker. 'We couldn't get clearance on the Chris Parker piece, so we had to yank it and bump up the dating service feature.'

'Excuse me?' Becker was already sweating under the lights: now he could feel the hairs beginning to prickle on the back of his neck.

Jake wrinkled his nose. 'Look Arnie – I know this is short notice, and nobody expects you to be letter-perfect on a cold reading – okay?'

'Okay hell!' Becker said, half under his breath, feeling the sweat beginning to gum up on his upper lip.

Jake swept on, all casual and friendly, like the salesman explaining why the new car won't start first time: 'You've got the copy in front of you – and it's also on the teleprompter . . .'

'Hey wait a minute?' The full horror of what the little man was saying was just making its impact. 'I can't just . . .'

At that moment the floor manager appeared, head encased in earphones and signalling like one of those flagmen on a carrier deck. 'Ten seconds to floor!'

'Break a leg,' Jake shouted enigmatically; then turned and yelled behind him, 'All right, settle down, people!' He gave Becker a final perky grin and scuttled away. Becker sat frozen, sweating, aghast.

The floor manager boomed: 'Three . . . two . . . one . . .'

Uplifting theme music swelled all round them. Julie Rayburn moistened her enamel lips and smiled like a cute tiger into the eye of the camera:

'Dating services! Sometimes it seems' – her bright eyes flitted almost imperceptibly with the rolling teleprompter, her come-hither voice emphasising the words at short lilting

78

intervals, apparently at random – 'there are more of them than there are single people in L.A. They promise romance – but do they deliver? For the story – sitting in for vacationing Steve Graham – is prominent Los Angeles attorney, Arnold Becker.' She turned: '*Arnie!*'

Through a dazzling blur Becker saw a red light on a camera wink on. There was a terrible silence. The longest silence Becker had ever known. As long as it takes a drowning man to recall his whole life, it seemed. Oh God, he thought. They'd all be watching. Roxanne, Stuart, Ann Kelsey, Castroverti – and Susan Bloom, like the chief eunuch in the harem... And what about Leland and Douglas? Would they be watching too – watching his shame? For his shame would be their shame...

He sat up and smiled, straight into camera. Then he began to speak. Or more accurately, he began to read – his lips jumping like little yoyos along the jerking lines of the teleprompter – his words coming in halting bunches, stiff and unnatural, as though he were speaking in a foreign language.

'What exactly are you ... buying when you go to ... a dating service? If the ads are to be ... believed, you're buying happiness ... romance ... love' – each phrase seemed glued to his parched lips, while the floor manager leapt about as though he were conducting the finale of Beethoven's Ninth: '*Faster! faster...!*'

The light on the camera winked off. Becker removed his earpiece and began inelegantly to massage his sore ear; as he did so he glimpsed a dark young woman on a nearby monitor-screen, her face registering exasperation and stony disapproval. She was the next presenter, awaiting her cue and Becker was watching the first spontaneous critic of his T.V. debut.

The next moment her face had brightened; she smiled into the screen and the whole studio now filled with her caustic, telly-trained voice that sounded as if it could cut glass:

'One was for a 75-year-old plumber – another, a guy who'd done time in San Quentin . . .'

Arnie Becker wanted to plunge his head in his hands, but was terrified the camera would catch him. Instead, he sat transfixed like a rabbit caught in the glare of headlights.

'. . . Number Three,' the woman on the monitor was saying, 'didn't quite speak English. I think he came from Mars . . .'

Becker grabbed at a glass of water, then sat dabbing a handkerchief to his sweating, pancaked brow. He tried to stay calm. He sat back and replaced the handkerchief in his breast pocket, like a corporation chief surveying a conference of top executives. He became so calm he failed to notice the monitor screen had suddenly switched on to him. His earpiece was still on the desk, like a pink snail.

The floor manager whispered deafeningly into a headset mike: '*Arnie? You're on! Arnie!*'

But Arnie Becker heard nothing. 'Arnie!' The floor manager began signalling, waving – launching a whole deck-full of F-111s into his dazzling night sky. Becker watched him, puzzled, then fascinated, mesmerised. He wondered if this extraordinary man with the headphones might somehow be part of the show? He leant forward, peering intently down at him.

Beside him, Julie Rayburn – the smile frozen like ice on

her pouting lips – said briskly, 'Arnie – let's open up the phones and take a call, shall we?'

Suddenly the truth dawned – or rather, it flashed like sheet lightning. He lunged forward, grabbed up his earpiece – almost spilling the glass of water – as Julie Rayburn sat intoning: 'The number is 5 . . . 5 . . . 5 – 2 . . . 1 . . .'

Becker was beginning to gabble, half to himself: 'Right! – the phones! I knew that . . .'

In front of him the floor manager was crouched low, muttering into the studio mike: 'Okay – first caller wants to ask about insurance premiums.'

Becker, tapping his earpiece, repeated desperately: 'Okay, first caller wants to ask about insurance prem . . .' He caught himself too late: smiled bleakly into the camera and added: '*Uh* . . . Caller Number One, you're on the air. What can I do for you?' (*Oh God!* he thought: What if my mother's watching?)

A voice, like an alien's trapped in a far-off refrigerator, crackled in his ear: '*I forgot to pay my car insurance for a month – I just didn't have the money. It expired on September 13th, and I had an accident on October 3rd. Am I cov . . .*'

'No,' said Becker. 'Thanks for calling' – and cut him off. Then, with the loose abandon of a gambler who has lost everything, he faced the camera: 'So my advice to all dating-service customers is this: Before you put your name on the dotted line' – and he winked into the cruel little eye of the camera: – *Know what you're signing!* . . . Arnold Becker, for News at Noon. Julie . . .?'

He had turned to Julie, on his right, who was about to 'wrap up' the sequence, when Becker's gaze alighted on yet another extraordinary sight. The floor manager was standing behind the camera, just in front of Julie Rayburn, and seemed to be doing a series of exotic breathing exercises – pushing his hands straight out in front of him, then stretching them out at either side, as far as they would go, accompanied by a strange, agonised grimace, as though his muscles were tearing with the effort.

Julie Rayburn recognised at once the 'stretch' motions – calling for the performers to keep going, fill in time – and turned breezily back to Becker: 'Food for thought! Tell me, Arnie . . .'

Becker gaped at her, the blood draining from under his pancake make-up. He gave her a ghastly smile, wondering if she were by any chance a sadist, and waited for the next onslaught. When it came, it was by way of making a virtue out of near-calamity. Julie Rayburn started to flirt with him:

'Er – *Arnie?* Any chance some lucky girl wants to keep you *all to herself* tonight?' She cocked her head, smiling brilliantly, but with eyes still like ice: 'Seems somebody may have pulled your tape?'

Becker made a deep, strangled sound: 'Uh . . . no. No . . . not . . .' His eyes locked on to hers: and for a moment he saw them soften. He smiled. She smiled. He recognised this for what it was: flirtation. Contrived, improvised, utterly insincere, but flirtation all the same. This was something he understood, something he was good at – even if it might be in the privacy of two million people, including half the staff of McKenzie Brackman.

But what the hell? – they were used to it. They might even expect it of him. He suddenly felt reckless: leant sideways, crinkling his blue eyes, and said, 'I don't know she'd go so far as sabotage my first chance of being a T.V. star, Julie!'

'What are we missing, Arnie?'

She was good! he thought. And quite pretty too, if you wiped all the glitz and glitter from your mind's eye. He went on smiling, careful not to leer. 'Well, those are State secrets, Julie . . . But maybe, if you're into candlelight dinners . . . long walks by the ocean . . . midnight swims.' (Amazing how the old routines always worked!)

She loved it: lowered her head and gave a little cooing chuckle. 'Don't tell me that under that lawyerly suit, you're really a romantic, Arnie?'

'If by that you mean I believe every woman in the world has one special light in her eyes that can be seen by one special man –' (Oh boy! – he was actually beginning to enjoy himself now) – 'then I plead guilty as charged.' He raised his hands: '*Nolo contendre* – lock me up and throw away the key . . .?'

The floor manager gave a wry smile. 'Good save, Arnie! *Phew . . .!*'

Jake, the director, was more than relieved. He liked it. First trick to Susan Bloom.

Chapter Nine

In the gloomy panelled witness room of the Criminal Court in the County of Los Angeles, Elsa Chandler's two lawyers both knew her fate now swung in the balance.

She sat bowed and broken, her chin sunk on to her chest, her bony fingers, which showed her age, writhing frantically between the folds of a crumpled handkerchief. Her make-up had run so badly her face seemed beyond repair; her eyes now raw and dry, as though the tearducts were finally exhausted.

Elsa's voice was a husky, cracked whisper as she faced her two defenders, Van Owen and Mullaney. 'I know we're rehearsed – we've gone over it. But I can't do it!' She looked at them both, imploring, desperate. 'Please! There must be some kind of plea bargain? I'm guilty – I'll go to prison . . .'

Grace's reply was flat, without mercy: 'We have no case without you, Elsa. The prosecution has no reason to make a deal.'

Tommy leant forward, moving to touch the woman's shoulder. He spoke kindly: 'A lot of people get scared just before they take the stand. It goes away once you're up there.'

Elsa lowered her head again and began to sob. 'I let my

husband humiliate me. I let him . . . I let him – let him take away my dignity. How can I explain to all those people?'

Tommy looked vainly at Grace, but she gave him no response. He turned to Elsa and said gently, 'You don't have to explain. All you have to do is tell them. If you don't, then he hurts you again – even though he's dead.'

Elsa sniffed into her handkerchief, which was now a damp rag. 'I don't even know if I can get the words out.' Her voice was a barely audible gasp.

'We'll help,' Tommy said. 'You gotta trust us.'

There was still no response from Grace. Her face had that bruised, withdrawn look, her expression closed, drained. Perhaps her absolute lack of visible emotion was contagious: for a stillness also seemed to have come over her client. Elsa Chandler was suddenly calm. Touching a hand hopelessly to her ravaged face, she said, 'Look, I need a few minutes. I'm going to get some water.'

They watched her go, in silence, then Tommy said, 'You want me to take her testimony?'

Grace's eyes flickered for a moment like camera shutters; she looked dully at Tommy, as though she were coming out of a trance. It was not a good portent. 'What are you talking about?' she said, beginning to frown.

Tommy stood back. He'd seen this happen before to counsellors who were under stress. Unable to endure the tension of their clients' agony, they cut themselves off – divorced themselves from the reality of the proceedings, which they then treated as remotely as though they were part of some film. Maybe it was one way of keeping sane in this job – although of little comfort to the client.

'You're too detached,' he told Grace: 'You're not

connecting with her. If *you* don't feel her pain, nobody else will.'

But he was wrong. Grace felt Elsa Chandler's pain all right, but it was on the inside; she couldn't let go, couldn't risk letting it spill out. Grace Van Owen was also close to breaking-point.

*

Elsa Chandler spoke in a quiet, dead voice. Very carefully, in case she tripped over the words, or lost control and began to weep. She spoke just loud enough to be heard by judge and counsel, though at the back of the court they were becoming impatient and noisy. There was a murmuring and pushing; the court officials were standing poised, ready to intervene.

'It always started the same way. Something would make him angry . . . He wouldn't like what I cooked; the house wasn't clean enough . . . He'd yell at me. Then he'd slap me. I'd try to calm him down, but I could feel it coming. He'd lose control. It was like . . . Like he just couldn't hurt me enough.'

'Did you ever try to resist?' Grace asked her.

'Twice. The first time he split my lip, the second he hit me so hard I had concussion.'

'Why didn't you leave him?'

'Oh, I wanted to. I really wanted to! But then he'd apologise. He'd be so nice. Then it would start all over again. Last Christmas things got so bad, I thought maybe there was a chance he'd let me go. So I asked for a divorce.'

'How did he respond?'

'He threw me out of the house. He said he was going to teach me a lesson – that I could never hope to survive on my

own. Without him, I'd wind up homeless, on the street . . .'
She lowered her head and gave a little shudder. 'I slept in the
yard that night,' she said, with a tiny whimper that was only
audible in the first few rows of the court.

'Did things get worse after that?' Grace asked gently.

'Yes. I wasn't allowed to go anywhere without him . . .'

'Please try to speak up, Mrs Chandler,' Judge Green said,
leaning forward.

She looked up at him, as though in shock. 'Speak up,'
Grace repeated, fearful that the judge, by interrupting, had
broken the spell – that Elsa Chandler had lost the
momentum and would never regain it.

'Where was I?' she asked, staring desperately down at
Grace.

'You were telling us how he never allowed you to go
anywhere without him,' Grace told her.

Elsa Chandler swallowed hard and nodded. 'Yes. He'd
call up several times a day to make sure I was there. I was
a prisoner.'

Grace faced her, with a sudden severity that would either
save or break the woman. 'Mrs Chandler – what happened
in the twenty-four hours prior to your husband's death?'

For some strange reason – a quirk of human nature, a
last desperate reserve of strength, of defiance against the
man who had forced her to sink so low – Elsa Chandler
raised her voice and this time spoke clearly, vibrantly, so
that even the dullest slouch at the back of the court could
hear every word she said. It was the voice of a woman
defeated, broken, now fighting for her life:

'The night before, Ralph was drinking. He called me into
his study. He made me sit down – then grabbed me by the
throat and put a gun to my head. He told me to look at the

87

clock . . . told me we were playing a game. He said there was one bullet in the gun, and six chambers. When the clock chimed the hour, he was going to pull the trigger. Either I'd die . . . or I'd live for another sixty minutes.'

There was a low, excited murmur across the whole court. The judge ignored it. Grace said, 'And he pulled the trigger?'

'Yes.'

'How many times?'

'Four times. Four hours. Till he passed out.'

There was another murmur, louder this time. Judge Green raised his head, but still did not intervene. When the sound had quietened, Grace said, 'And he continued to abuse you next morning, didn't he?'

'I was sleeping,' the woman said. 'I woke up and found . . . there was pain shooting through my whole body. It was like I was being torn apart!'

'What was he doing?'

Suddenly Elsa Chandler was silent. It was as though the memory had paralysed her power of speech.

'I know this is hard,' Grace said, 'but we need to know. What was he doing?'

The silence was total. Terrible. Grace said, 'He was sodomising you, wasn't he?'

'*Objection!*' Graphia was out of his chair like a jack-in-the-box. 'She's leading the witness!'

'Sustained.'

Elsa Chandler looked at Grace like a distraught, terrified child. And Grace looked back, like a desperate mother straining to reach the child, comfort her, reassure her. When she spoke, her voice was calm – with the controlled calm of somebody who knows that with one wrong word, one false note, the game is lost. The woman's *life* is lost. 'What was he doing?' she asked.

'He was . . . He was sodomising me with . . . He was doing it with the wooden handle of a hairbrush. After he left, I tried to get up. There was blood all over the bed.'

'When did you next hear from your husband?'

'About seven that evening. He called me from his office. He ordered me to get over there and bring him his gun.'

'What happened when you got to your husband's office?'

'He screamed at me that I was late. He said to give him the gun. I took it out of my purse . . . and he stood up . . . stood up . . .'

'And then what happened?'

'I shot him.' For a moment there was a bleak silence, then she collapsed – her whole body slumping forward against the rail, her face in her hands, her shoulders wracked with sobs. 'I didn't mean to,' – the words were barely intelligible – 'but I knew he was going to kill me! *I knew he was going to kill me!*'

'Thank you. No further questions.'

*

Graphia rose, looking vaguely discomfited. 'How did you *know*, Mrs Chandler?'

'What?'

'How did you know he was going to kill you?' No answer. 'How did you *know* your husband was going to kill you at that moment?' Still no answer. 'Did he say so?'

'No . . .'

'Did he move towards you?'

'No. But I knew he would . . .'

'But he never *did*? Did he?'

'No.'

Graphia paused, lowering his eyes a moment. Elsa had managed to struggle up, to compose himself slightly. She waited for the next question like a dog anticipating a blow.

'You claim you were a prisoner for twelve years. But you never told a friend – never told any member of your family. You never called the police. Did you?'

'Ralph said if I did, he'd kill me.'

'Mrs Chandler,' Graphia said, raising his eyes to meet hers, 'you're still living in that prison, aren't you?'

She stared at him. 'I don't know what you mean?'

'I'm referring, Mrs Chandler, to the 5.3 million dollar house your husband bought in 1989. He's been dead almost a year – but you still live there.'

'Yes.'

'Aren't the memories too painful?'

Grace cut in: 'Argumentative, Your Honour?'

'Sustained.'

'How much money, Mrs Chandler, did you spend on clothes prior to your husband's death?'

'I don't know.'

'Your department store charges alone total twenty-six-thousand dollars,' said Graphia.

'Ralph made me buy clothes. He liked to show off his money . . .'

'What a monster,' Graphia said, with icy understatement. 'What an awful thing to do! He made you buy clothes.'

Grace was on her feet. 'This is abusive!'

'Sustained,' said Judge Green. 'Watch yourself, Mr

Graphia.' (The court, especially the reporters, were loving it.)

'You did other things with your husband's money, too, didn't you, Mrs Chandler? You gave twenty thousand dollars to your lover, Steven Waering . . .'

'*Objection!*' cried Grace, while Elsa sobbed, 'He wasn't my lover . . .!'

'Sustained,' said Judge Green.

'I never . . .' – Elsa was struggling for words like a drowning woman gasping for air – 'We never . . . slept together. He was the only person who understood . . .'

'Mrs Chandler,' Graphia said haughtily, 'if it was really so terrible, why didn't you just leave the night your husband locked you out?'

'I couldn't. I was too ashamed.'

'Oh, come on! You're a grown woman. You could have walked to a neighbour's house. You could have called Mr Waering. Why didn't you?' There was no answer. '*Why didn't you*, Mrs Chandler?'

'I didn't have anything on!' She was staring down at the smooth, self-confident D.A.A., her eyes wild. 'Don't you understand? He tore my nightgown off and threw me out! I couldn't . . . I couldn't go anywhere! I couldn't let anyone see me. *I was naked!*'

*

In his office, Arnie Becker was sitting demurely next to Roxanne on the visitors' couch. He sounded mildly desperate: 'I tell you, Rox, I kept hoping for the San Andreas Fault to open up right under the studio! There was this big spotlight above me, and I thought, one big jolt and it's over . . .'

Roxanne patted his hand indulgently. 'Arnie, they switched the copy on you at the last minute. *Anybody* – even an old pro – could've missed a couple of cues.'

'I felt my mouth was full of cotton. The words lost their meaning – it was like reading Esperanto – I didn't know what I was even saying!'

Roxanne gave him a sly, sideways glance. 'You managed to do okay with Julie Rayburn.'

Becker held both hands up. 'Okay – shoot me now!'

'Arnie . . .'

'It was reflex, Rox – I swear it! I just went on to autopilot.' He was even waving his arms now, floundering in abject excuses – but at the same time, trawling pretty widely for compliments, even if they were only backhand ones. 'I mean, I was coughing blood up there – I just had to do *something*!'

Fortunately for him, Roxanne had decided to be magnanimous. She smiled and said, 'Well, it was your first time. Don't be too hard on yourself.'

Becker had a sudden, dreadful thought – the same he'd had in the heat of battle last night. 'You don't think my mother was watching, do you?'

As he spoke, there was a tap at the door. Susan Bloom's secretary put her head round: 'Arnie? Tony Berkman for you – the producer from K.C.Y.B.'

Becker sank his head in his hands. 'Tell him I died.'

'He knows. He was there.' Her head disappeared again, the door closed. Becker looked bleakly at Roxanne. 'You see? You see what I have to put up with here?' He stood up wearily and reached for the phone, picking it up as though it weighed fifty pounds. 'Tony? Hi! Man, I am so . . .!' There was an acute pause. 'They did . . .?' *She did . . .!* He put his hand over the mouthpiece and whispered loudly to Roxanne: 'He says they got almost two hundred phone calls – all from women – asking if I was coming back!'

'Who's the "she"?' Roxanne asked.

'Julie Rayburn. She thinks I might have a *huge* TVQ.'

'I'm sure she does,' Roxanne said drily.

Becker was speaking eagerly into the phone: 'No, no! That's terrific, Tony, I . . .! Really? What about Steve Graham . . .? Uh-huh . . . uh . . . huh. Well, I guess . . . yeah, I guess I could *make* the time. What kind of money are we talking here?'

Roxanne gave a little inward sigh and thought, Here we go – *superstar!*

*

'Elsa Chandler killed her husband.' Assistant District Attorney Jim Graphia's final argument to the Criminal Court was delivered in a tone somewhere between that of a practised orator and a company chairman running through the annual accounts. He managed to sound both menacing and humdrum in the same breath.

'She killed her husband. No-one disputes that. She went to his office, she pulled out a gun, she shot him in cold blood. She claims it was self-defence – that she was a battered wife – that she was abused and degraded by Ralph Chandler for twelve years. Yet strangely, ladies and gentlemen' – he turned, sweeping an elegant hand toward the jury – 'she told no-one. Not a friend, not her family, not the police. The only person who corroborates her story is

Steven Waering, the man she was seeing behind her husband's back – the man to whom she gave twenty thousand dollars.'

He paused. The jury looked from Graphia to Elsa Chandler. Always a bad sign.

'The question is – *was* Elsa Chandler abused by her husband. I doubt it. But even if you believe she was – even if you think Ralph Chandler deserved to die – there is no law that justifies what Mrs Chandler did. There is no law that allows a woman to kill her husband in revenge for past abuse, or to protect herself from future abuse.' He leant forward slightly, spelling it out for the jury: 'It's self-defence if – and only if – Elsa Chandler's life was in immediate danger. And it wasn't, ladies and gentlemen. Ralph Chandler was twenty-six feet away from her, behind a desk. He hadn't hit her. He hadn't even moved towards her. But Elsa Chandler shot him anyway.'

Graphia paused, stepped back, looked hard at Elsa Chandler, then back to the jury. 'She could've called the police. She didn't. She could have gone to a friend. She didn't. She didn't make any of those choices. No. Instead, she chose to kill another human being.' He paused again, his voice low and methodical. 'The law says Elsa Chandler is guilty of murder.'

When he sat down, there were probably not many people in that courtroom who disagreed with Assistant District Attorney Graphia. Grace knew it in her bones, as she rose to make a final speech for the defence. She felt she had a mountain to climb, and very little time in which to do it.

She began slowly: 'The first time Ralph Chandler beat his wife was on her twenty-eighth birthday. Ralph was particular about the way she looked and she wanted to please him, so she spent the day getting ready. She picked out the perfect dress and decided to try a new hairstyle.

'Ralph Chandler walked in that night – and he called his wife a whore. He ordered her never to change her appearance again without his permission. And then he hit her – over and over again – until Mrs Chandler lost consciousness. She woke up in agony – only to find that her husband had cut off all her hair.

'For twelve years Elsa Chandler endured this kind of abuse. She was trapped in an endless cycle of violence, terror, rape and battery. Ladies and gentlemen, when these things happen in our society, most of us want to turn away. We want, somehow, to believe it was the victim's fault. Why didn't she leave? we ask. Why didn't she tell someone? Ladies and gentlemen, Elsa Chandler didn't do any of these things for a very simple reason. *She knew that her husband would kill her if she did.* And it wasn't just a threat! He forced her to rehearse her own death.'

Grace had the whole court hanging on every word now. All she had to do was keep up the momentum. Just as long as she didn't falter – didn't lose them . . .

'Mrs Chandler knew what her husband planned that night. He'd been promising to do it for twelve years. She was going to die. He was finally going to kill her.' Grace paused, turned and surveyed the whole courtroom, then looked towards the jury. 'Yes, ladies and gentlemen, Elsa Chandler *did* have a choice. She chose to live. She's not a criminal. She's a human being who was tortured nearly to death. And in that final moment, she found the will to survive. Please, don't punish her for it.'

This time the whole jury was looking at Grace.

Chapter Ten

The Los Angeles Probate Court was in final session. Judge Myron Swaybill had reached his conclusions in the case of Riley, and this morning he was not going to waste more time than necessary in delivering them.

'In reviewing the records of this trial,' he began, 'as well as the Government files, I've concluded that the evidence is sufficient to overcome the presumption of death and to justify the conclusion that Captain Riley *may still be alive.*' He turned to Sean Riley, who was concealing his obvious relief and delight with modest dignity.

'Therefore, Mr Riley,' the judge went on, 'I'm refusing to declare your father dead.'

From the younger brother, however, came a loud hiss of outrage. Mike Riley's thin angry lips framed a vivid obscenity, as he flashed a venemous look at Judge Swaybill who behaved as though he hadn't noticed. Beside Riley Jr. sat his fiancée, a pale, conventionally pretty girl, dressed as though for church. She leaned closer to him, squeezing his thin arm in both her hands.

The judge now went on to address the brothers together, impartially:

'In the matter of your mother's estate I have no choice. I direct that a trust be established and that Sean Riley be named trustee. He may use the money, under this court's supervision, to look for your father.' He paused, his eyes moving across both brothers' faces. 'My ruling notwithstanding,' he added, ' it saddens me that the Vietnam war continues to divide your family. I sincerely hope that you can both now find a way to be brothers again.'

'Amen to that!' Sean Riley said, under his breath.

'This case is adjourned.'

*

It was a curious anticlimax. Judge Swaybill had left. Rollins and Jane Maxon were busy collecting their papers. Their work was done. Jane nodded her congratulations to her colleague, and prepared to leave.

Mike Riley was alone. Odd, because he was the only one in the courtroom who had company to enjoy – a loyal companion who shared all the agony of his disappointment. Yet he was still alone. The terrible, self-imposed isolation that had dogged him since childhood, and from which he'd believed, for these few brief days in court, he might be rescued by the comforts of money and marraige . . . Now dashed away, in a few stark sentences. And the fact that the father he'd never seen was now pronounced – officially, judicially – 'still alive', made his isolation complete.

He looked suddenly deflated, his anger and bitterness sapped. Depression would now set in – a gnawing depression that had beset him since his earliest awareness, and

97

would be followed, as day follows night, by the old soul-destroying resentment.

His fiancée wouldn't know this: she'd stand by him, closing him off, helping to lock the resentment away so that it could only feed on itself. Rollins knew it, but it was none of his business. Jane Maxon probably knew it, but didn't feel there was much more she could do, except discuss further points of law with a view to an appeal.

And Sean Riley knew it. He now stepped up to them both, as they reached the door, and made to touch his brother on the arm. Mike Riley flinched away, avoiding Sean's eyes.

'If you change your mind,' Sean said, 'I could use your help.'

'I don't think so.' Mike Riley put his arm round his fiancée and started towards the door.

His elder brother tried again: 'Mike – I never wanted to cut you off . . . I'll try to get you something . . .'

Mike Riley turned, angrily. 'You still don't get it, do you?' He shook his head. 'It wasn't about the money. It was *never* about the money.' He turned away again, holding his fiancée close to him; and Sean watched them both walk out.

Rollins, who had witnessed this little scene, hung back saying nothing. Deep down, he had never been wholly sure of his client's case – had always considered it a chance of a hundred-to-one, perhaps more like a thousand-to-one, that Captain James Riley were still alive. But there was one thing of which Rollins was now absolutely sure. Judge Myron Swaybill had made the right decision.

*

Susan Bloom had her feet up on the desk and was juggling with two telephones when Roxanne marched into her office. The cigarette smoke was so dense, Roxanne could hardly breathe at first.

Bloom gave her wide, vapid smile, whilst talking into one of the phones: 'You know what I'm saying, Jerry. Beef has no intention of being another Stallone. Rambo is too cardboard. he only wants to play real people.' She cupped a claw-like hand over the phone and mouthed to Roxanne: 'Be right with you!' Back into the phone: 'So it's Predator with a sensitive side. Is he the lead? Great! Send it over.'

The door opened and a swarthy man with a face like a well-groomed rat poked his snout round the door. 'Fox is on Two,' he said, in a tight little Hollywood go-get-'em voice. 'And they're still holding your table at Spago's.'

Bloom waved her cigarette at him. 'I'm on my way up, Scottie. Tell Fox I'll call him back . . .'

Roxanne said, 'We had an appointment.'

Into the second phone, Bloom said, 'Wally, I'm still tied up – I'll call you back . . .' She slammed the phone down, said into the first, 'Jerry, I got somebody . . . yeah, yeah . . .' Roxanne was standing directly over her now. The woman's scent, combined with the cigarette fumes, were making her feel sick.

Bloom, still holding the first phone to her ear, said, without removing the cigarette, 'What can I do for you?' – and continued into the phone: 'If we can get together on the back end, she's yours. And love to Billy! Get back to you, Jerry . . .' She punched a button on the phone, said, 'Tell Fox I'll call back. And hold the rest off . . . I know – just do

99

it . . .' She finally hung up. 'What can I do for you?' she said again, breathing in two lungfuls of smoke.

'You have to notify us when you hold a press conference,' Roxanne said stolidly. 'You can't smoke in the halls – you don't tip the building staff – and please remember the photocopier is for everybody.'

Bloom waved her cigarette. 'Fair enough. Anything else?'

Roxanne swallowed hard. 'I know you're used to working on your own but . . . Fair enough?'

Susan Bloom removed her feet from the desk and sprawled back so that the designer chair took her whole weight. Roxanne was amazed it didn't crack under her. 'Honey,' she began – pure Tinsel-Town now, all teeth and fake sincerity, like Nixon on a bad day – 'my life goes about a hundred miles an hour. That makes me inconsiderate sometimes, but I'm not a monster. If I've been offensive, I'm sorry. I appreciate you pointing it out.'

'You do?' said Roxanne, truly surprised.

'Uh-huh! I liked your style, too. You're direct without being obnoxious. I hear you came up from the ranks?'

Roxanne swallowed again, uncomfortably aware that her wholesome 'girl-from-the-prairie' look was no match for raw Hollywood. 'I used to work for Arnold Becker,' she said meekly.

Susan Bloom smiled like an over-fed jackal. 'What kind of deal do you have now?' – she waved her cigarette like a semaphore – 'Bumps? Fringes? Points? You know. What are they putting up to retain your talent?'

Roxanne stared at her. 'I never thought of it as talent,' she murmured.

'You should!' Bloom cried. 'Good office managers are

scarcer than hens' teeth.' She hauled herself to her feet. 'I'm late for lunch. But you and I – we got to have a heart-to-heart sometimes.' She reached out and shook Roxanne's hand; her fingers felt like a wood rasp. 'It's been a pleasure!' She had a fresh cigarette alight, waving it towards the coffee machine, and Roxanne noticed coffee was oozing from its base on to deep-pile carpet. 'Help yourself to cappuccino, honey!'

*

'Has the jury reached its verdict?'

Judge Green's words were dropped into a packed, deafening silence. You could hear several hundred people holding their breath: the reporters crowded together at the end of the Press benches, ready to make a run for the phones; Grace Van Owen sitting very pale and straight; beside her, Tommy Mullaney, slouched and deceptively relaxed. While between them Elsa Chandler just sat. It was as though all emotion had been squeezed out of her, like a husk of dead fruit.

The foreman of the jury intoned the response: 'We have, Your Honour!' He handed the slip of folded paper down to the court official, who carried it over to Judge Green. He opened it, read it, folded it again and handed it to the clerk.

The clerk spoke in the mournful tones of the public servant: 'In the matter of the People versus Elsa Chandler, on the charge of first-degree murder, we find the defendant – not guilty.'

It was as though the air had gone out of a balloon. A spontaneous roar of applause went up, and there was a stampede for the doors. Grace Van Owen let out a deep, exhausted sigh, and her hand closed over Elsa Chandler's. The woman didn't react in any way.

'It's over,' Grace whispered to her. But she didn't move – her eyes were glazed, her hands cold. She was already dead inside.

Judge Green was saying, in a business-like voice: 'Members of the jury, thank you for your service. We're adjourned. The defendant is free to go.'

It was like the end of a play. The curtain had come down, the audience was anxious to go home. All except a group of reporters who now surrounded Grace and Elsa, like jackals round a fresh carcass.

Elsa saw them and shuddered. 'Do I have to face them?' she asked, in a tiny, cracked voice.

'Not the questions – Tommy and I'll take those,' Grace said quickly, as the pack came closing in.

Just then, from the main body of the courtroom, there appeared the handsome, soberly-dressed figure of Steven Waering. He was smiling nervously but carried himself well. Grace had entertained serious misgivings about him; but now, seeing him stand close to Elsa and put his arm protectively around her, she was relieved to be proved wrong. Besides, Grace no longer had the strength to support Elsa – even in her hour of triumph. Thank God for Waering!

The reporters were all round now, yelling their inane, staccato questions, as though the secrets of all deep human drama and tragedy could be fitted into a couple of snappy sound-bites: '*How do you feel to be free, Mrs Chandler?*' '*Did you expect to be freed?*'

Grace looked at Tommy, who grinned grimly back at her. 'They're all yours, Grace.' He was pleased – very pleased – for Elsa. But he still thought the woman had been damned lucky. It wasn't the way he'd have played it. He didn't believe in gambling with the law.

'*What did you reckon your client's chances were, Miss Van Owen? Her real chances . . .?*'

*

Tommy looked up slowly as Grace walked into his office. He was leaning back in his old comfortable chair, his hands cradling the back of his neck. He waited for her to speak.

'I wanted to thank you,' she said.

'It wasn't me. It was you.'

'I was lucky.'

'That, too,' he said, loosening his hands, and sat forward. 'You risked her life, Grace. Just so you could have something to hold on to. So you could prove you're still one hell of a lawyer.'

She hung her head, and for a moment stood there in front of him like a contrite schoolgirl. Tommy nodded. 'And you did it. You won.'

There was a long pause. 'It's not enough,' she said.

Mullaney looked at her, then nodded. 'I know. Believe me, Grace – I *know* . . .'

103

Chapter Eleven

Douglas Brackman was not going to let a little trouble with Susan Bloom disturb his day. On the evening of the Chandler acquittal he had dinner with an old friend from law school days – fellow L.A. attorney, Robert Caporale. Brackman hadn't seen him for nearly a year, after Bob Caporale had gone to work as a tax consultant for the San Diego Chamber of Commerce. Then, a couple of weeks ago, they'd run into each other in the Athletic Club on Beverly, and had been meeting fairly regularly for meals ever since.

Brackman, a naturally reserved man, didn't boast many close friends. Bob Caporale certainly wasn't an intimate, but their relationship went back a long way. Both were successful lawyers, both securely married with children, both had a passion for the niceties of U.S. Company Law, and each was a devoted follower of American football and Italian opera. For, in this city of barbarian tastes, where the barbarians had all the money and thus called the shots, Brackman liked to feel there was a small, private sanctum in his life where he could draw on the wholesome, manly strengths of traditional sport and high culture. His companion in this sanctum was Bob Caporale.

They were dining in a discreet, crowded restaurant off Sunset, the walls on three sides lined with the dark, varnished ends of huge wine barrels. The tables were large and well-spaced, each with its white, hand-laundered linen with lace borders, a pair of deep red velvet wing chairs, solid silver candlesticks, silver cutlery and heavy crystal wine goblets. The place was Bob Caporale's choice, and he was doing the honours. Douglas was preparing to enjoy himself. This was the finest place they'd hit so far, since he and his friend had started on these little dining-out sessions.

A tall, stiff *maitre d'*, who looked like a stand-in for Rhett Butler, bent solicitously behind Caporale's shoulder. 'The saddle of lamb is excellent, m'sieur,' he murmured, pointing a little gold pencil at the enormous, handwritten menu card. 'Not too heavy, and quite beautiful, *á point* . . .'

'That okay for you, Doug?' Caporale enquired, raising his dark glossy eyebrows.

'Sounds just fine,' Brackman agreed. Who was he, humble attorney-at-law, to question such munificence?

His companion ordered, the *maitre d'* bowed, discreet smiles were exchanged. Caporale was about Brackman's age, late forties, less balding but beginning to run slightly to fat, with a well-sculptured profile.

Brackman had taken his first bite into a brittle sliver of melba toast which he ate to the accompaniment of a succulent lump of *paté de foie gras*. It was so delicious, he felt he was committing some deep sin. 'Hmmmm!' he murmured, with uncharacteristic abandon.

Bob Caporale beamed. 'I knew you'd appreciate it!'

'I give it a five-point-eight rating,' Brackman said,

nodding judiciously round. 'Must be the best-kept secret in town, this place?'

His dinner guest gave him a small, secret smile. He paused, then took a deep breath. 'Douglas, there's a reason why I wanted to have dinner here . . .'

'Sure – aren't we celebrating?' Brackman said, chewing luxuriously. 'My citation from the Bar – yes?'

Bob Caporale lifted his glass of pink *kir*: 'A well-deserved honour, Douglas! But also, I needed to discuss something personal.'

'Fire away,' Brackman said. 'What are friends for?'

'Douglas, I'm gay.'

*

Brackman felt as though he had swallowed his entire plate – and that it had got stuck half way down. '*What?*' he said, choking. He grabbed for a heavy napkin the size of a pillowcase and dabbed it desperately against his lips.

'I'm gay,' Bob Caporale repeated.

'Bob – *please* . . .' Brackman said, almost in a whisper, and glanced nervously round.

'It's no secret!' Caporale laughed. '*Not in here* . . .'

A slightly queasy look had crept over Brackman's austere features. In his innocence, he had noticed only the period opulence of the restaurant – the rich decor, the lavish tableware. He had neglected the clientele. For a top attorney, he was a remarkably unobservant man. He now began surveying the restaurant with a more careful, suspicious eye. Almost every table was taken by couples – *male* couples. Then, at one table near the corner, he caught the reassuring sight of a woman. Then a second woman –

106

leaning over now, in Brackman's line of vision, to light her partner's cigarette. *Oh God*, he thought. He was growing up fast!

'I know it's a shock,' Caporale went on, 'hearing it like this ... Or perhaps it isn't? Evelyn had suspected it for years.'

'*Evelyn?*' In his confusion, Brackman had forgotten all about the former *Mrs* Caporale. 'You mean, you told your Ex?' he said, too far off guard now even to try and cover his shock.

'I wasn't sure how the kids would handle it ...' the other said earnestly, as though he were discussing a mildly controversial point of law.

'*You told your kids?*' Brackman stared in bleak amazement at his companion across the table. He was beginning to feel punch-drunk.

'I want to tell everyone who's close to me,' Caporale said, staring his friend in the eye. Brackman couldn't help wincing.

'Why are you telling *me*, Bob?' he asked, feeling a sudden lurch of unease deep in his stomach.

'Because you're my oldest friend,' Caporale said, as though it were the most obvious fact in the world. 'I've always admired you, Douglas ...'

Oh no! thought Brackman. *It's going to be a declaration of love* ... He sat gripping his fork as though it were a weapon, and knew that he had turned deathly pale.

Bob Caporale went on, apparently oblivious of his friend's reaction, 'I've admired you, Doug – ever since we were both room-mates in our freshman year ...'

'Now hold on!' said Brackman. He was vaguely, uncomfortably aware that his domed forehead had started to

107

sweat. 'Are you trying to say, Bob, that through all the years we've known each other . . .?

'I didn't even admit it myself for a long time,' Caporale said, his voice dead earnest, although he had a slight smile now on his full lips.

Brackman laid down his fork and leant forward across the table, speaking almost in a whisper, 'Now listen, Bob. I'd like to get one thing perfectly clear. For myself, our friendship has always been a strictly heterosexual' – he hesitated, as though the very word, in the luxurious intimacy of this place, was a sacrilege – 'a strictly heterosexual *male bonding*,' he went on, groping awkwardly for the words. 'I'm sorry, Bob – but I am not interested in being propositioned . . .'

'I'm not propositioning you,' the other said gently, the smile still holding. 'I'm not attracted to you.'

Brackman tried to swallow and said, 'Oh' – it came out more like a throttled belch.

'I only wanted you to know because . . . because it's just who I am. I just hope you can accept it?'

At that moment, they were mercifully interrupted by a handsome, dark-eyed wine waiter who had stopped at Caporale's elbow and smiled sweetly, showing him the bottle of Chardonnay wrapped in a napkin that reminded Brackman of a tiny shroud. 'Is that all right, m'sieur?' he murmured.

'I'm sure it's fine!' Caporale said, returning the smile. Then he looked round and smiled again at Brackman.

Brackman waited till the young wine waiter had poured their goblets full, watched as Caporale tasted his and nodded enthusiastically, then took what he hoped was not an ostentatious gulp himself – wishing it were straight rye.

'Well, certainly,' he said, as the waiter withdrew, 'it's our right, Bob.'

'And I hope you'll meet my lover Bill,' Caporale went on. We're planning a Fall wedding. It would mean a lot to me ⁝ you'd agree to be my best man again – second time ound.'

Second time round, Brackman thought, taking another ulp of wine. He must be careful not to get drunk, he hought. The world might be going crazy, but at all costs, Douglas Brackman, attorney-at-law, must not get drunk.

*

.fterwards, Brackman couldn't remember how he got rough the rest of the meal, except, having made his nomentous declaration, Bob had seemed content to fall ack on an almost ponderously normal line of small talk. his Brackman followed with eager compliance, like a nountain climber following his guide after having nego-ated a particularly perilous slope.

They talked about the high cost of civil litigation in the os Angeles county courts; the quirks and foibles of articular judges; recited the results and anecdotes of arious cases they'd recently been on. By the time the coffee nd *crèmes brulées* arrived, Caporale was his old genial self: arrulous, informative, mildly witty – and perfectly relaxed.

Douglas watched, dead sober, as his friend signed the neque. He was an obvious habitué here, and Brackman ondered how the waiters judged *him* – Caporale's old uddy from college and law school days.

By the time they got outside, Brackman felt as though e'd just completed a heavy case – with a hung jury. The experience had left him drained, as though the shock had anaesthetised him against the effects of alcohol. Thank God he wasn't driving. He needed some air.

*

Douglas watched as the valet-parking attendant brought his friend's trim little Japanese coupé up on to the forecourt, waved Caporale goodnight and started walking briskly out under the palms towards the Strip. He heard the little car's tyres sizzle past him and raised a hand in parting farewell, trying to keep the stiff smile plastered across his face. Then somebody bumped into him. Hard. He could feel the packed muscle of the man's weight against his shoulder, and felt himself stumble off the kerb.

'Sorry,' he muttered. The passer-by suddenly turned and gave him a forceful shove.

'*Yeah!* – you're gonna be sure sorry – *sucker!*' The next moment Brackman felt himself hurled bodily back into the shadow of the palms.

'*What in the – !*' he began, and felt his jacket seized by the lapels. He could hear the two thousand dollar fabric beginning to tear, and for a brief, terrifying moment was forced to stare, eyeball-to-eyeball, into a dark, sweaty brutal face, the lips stretched back from the teeth, the whole expression one of concentrated, unreasoning hatred . . .

'Keep your fag-face outta here – *goddam queer . . .!*'

Afterwards, Douglas remembered the face being made even more horrible by the faint greenish glow of the restaurant sign somewhere behind the palms. It gave his assailant's features an eerie, unnatural look, like something out of a horror film. Then something that felt like the front of a freight train collided with his jaw; he saw an arm jack back and shoot out again like a steam-piston and felt the clear, sickening crunch of cartilege breaking somewhere deep in his nose. Then the freight train crashed into his solar plexus and the air went out of his body in a screaming whine. Brackman felt the hard cold pavement come swimming up and slamming against his face. And then bright, exploding blackness.

*

'In addition to the broken nose, he suffered facial lacerations, bruising and a cracked rib.' Leland McKenzie spoke in the flat tones of muted outrage; and there was a sharp intake of breath round the conference table.

'Oh my God!' Ann Kelsey cried.

'How much did they get?' said Becker.

'Robbery was apparently not the motive,' McKenzie said. 'He had two hundred dollars in his wallet when he was admitted to Cedars.'

There was a stunned silence. 'Where did this happen?' C.J. Lamb said at last.

'On the Westside. Outside a restaurant' – McKenzie consulted his notes – 'place called "Androcles".'

'"*Androcles?*"' C.J.'s lovely eyes widened; she hoped her surprise hadn't shown.

Leland McKenzie peered at her over his bifocals. 'You know the place?' he said quietly.

The English girl had had time to resume a poker-face. 'Rings a bell,' she murmured.

Arnie Becker had sat up, frowning. 'Hey wait a minute –' he began, then seemed to think better of it.

111

'Yes, Arnie?' McKenzie was looking at him, waiting.

'Ah, it's nothing. Somewhere else I was thinking of,' Arnie said, with a little wave, just as Stuart Markowitz came to the rescue:

'Does that mean Douglas is going to miss his award luncheon?'

'I hope not,' McKenzie said. Beside him sat Roxanne, brisk and businesslike in her best business suit with slightly power-added shoulders – the one Arnie Becker said made her look unfeminine. Today, she had been asked by McKenzie to sit in for Brackman at conference.

'Poor Douglas,' she said, with genuine feeling. 'If his injuries are that bad, is there any chance of getting the luncheon put back?'

'Out of the question,' said McKenzie. 'These things are arranged months ahead. However, the doctors say if his condition remains stable, they'll let him come here tomorrow. So, in his absence, we'll keep this conference short.'

Roxanne flushed: she felt this a slight on her competence. 'But we can't expect him to appear with those injuries,' she protested, appalled that Leland could seem so callous. 'There'll be all the Press and photographers there . . .!'

'Have the Press got on to it yet?' asked Ann Kelsey.

'Better keep them out of it,' C.J. said emphatically, 'if it can possibly be arranged.'

Becker said, 'You can't keep 'em out of it. *I* should know. They're like vultures round a corpse . . .' He saw McKenzie look at him disapprovingly and mumbled, 'Not literally, of course.'

'Well thanks,' said Roxanne, glowering.

'Funny it wasn't a mugging,' said Markowitz. 'Press might make something of that.'

'Shouldn't we put out that it *was* a mugging?' Roxanne suggested. 'Or at least, an *attempted* mugging? It might put them off the scent.'

'Scent?' McKenzie said suspiciously.

Even as she'd spoken, Roxanne could have bitten off her tongue. 'Wondering why he wasn't at the luncheon to get his award,' she said hurriedly. 'I mean, I just can't bear the thought of him having to get up there in front of all those people with his face all bruised like that.'

Leland McKenzie was tapping his pencil impatiently on the table top. 'Let's just wait and see what the doctors say. Now – can we get started, Rox?'

'Good idea.' She bristled, squaring her padded shoulders but determined not to show her annoyance. It was bad enough having dear Douglas lying in hospital; what she certainly didn't need now was to be patronised by the Senior Partner in front of the whole firm – especially in front of Arnie.

She consulted her notes, then faced the table. 'Paul versus Humbolt Logging.'

McKenzie nodded. 'Ah yes – the sawmill accident.'

'I'm down to my last motion,' Ann Kelsey said.

Tommy Mullaney sprawled back and grinned at her. 'They gonna revoke your Sierra Club membership for defending loggers, Ann?' Tommy enjoyed the odd jibe at the discomforture of his colleagues when he perceived their 'politically correct' attitudes conflicting with their professional loyalties.

Ann Kelsey replied stiffly, 'This time the logging company isn't at fault. The tree-spiker caused the accident.'

'Moving on –' Roxanne said, not wanting to be accused

again of indulging conference in idle distractions; but Castroverti now chipped in:

'Tree-spiker?' he said, raising an eyebrow.

'Environmental activist,' Markowitz explained helpfully. 'They drive nails into trees to keep them from being cut down.'

'Activists?' snorted Becker. 'They're terrorists!'

'He's also our co-defendant,' Ann Kelsey said tartly, and a groan of sympathy went up from her fellow litigators round the table.

'What's his name?' McKenzie asked.

'Snyder,' said Ann Kelsey quickly; she was anxious to dispose of the subject.

'Not *Russ* Snyder!' Becker cried. 'Leader of the "Redwood Warriors"? – "Trees Before People" – burn all cars, tear up the roads and highways, and go live wild in the woods . . . That the one?'

'The same,' said Ann Kelsey.

'He's a nut,' Becker said. 'A tree-green fascist!'

Roxanne put both hands on the table and tried again: 'Now shall we –'

'I used to know the Snyder family,' McKenzie said ruminatively. The others listened dutifully as he went on: 'Old Jack Snyder made a fortune in gas stations during the auto-boom of the Fifties. I represented him once in a suit against the State Boundary Commission.' McKenzie sounded tired, nostalgic.

'Son's a rich kid?' Jonathan Rollins asked, glancing at Ann Kelsey.

'Seems so.' She shrugged. 'But money doesn't come into this one.'

'Like hell it doesn't,' Becker laughed. 'Guy flunks out of

114

college, doesn't have to work, and because there's no Vietnam for a grand-stand, he chooses trees.'

'Okay,' Roxanne persisted, 'moving on –'

Rollins interrupted again: 'I don't envy you this one, Ann.'

'Thanks for the encouragement, guys,' she said coldly, and slapped a hand down on her folder. 'Okay – now listen up! We're all clear on the agenda. Any questions?' She didn't wait for further interruptions. 'Then we're adjourned . . .'

Chapter Twelve

The defence table in the Los Angeles Civil Court was crowded, every inch of its surface stacked with files and documents. Ann Kelsey was seated next to the President of Humbolt Logging, Mr Eugene Etter – a massively-built man with a craggy, outdoor face and heavy moustache who looked very uncomfortable in his badly-fitting city suit.

On Ann Kelsey's other side was the co-defendant, Russ Snyder. He was a large, youngish man whose fleshy patrician features were partly masked by a big unkempt beard. His hair, like his beard, was thick and long, and did not look quite clean. These, together with his court attire – loose hunting jacket, patched jeans and mountain boots – were designed to create a rough 'proletarian' image – though a close observer would have quickly noticed, through the man's soft, educated voice and smooth hands, that this was no genuine horny-handed son of toil. Instead, Russ Snyder was the self-appointed leader and chief 'spokesperson' of the 'Redwood Warriors', one of those noisy, myriad pressure groups that spring up in response to the endless demand for fresh, fashionable public causes, and which then incubate under the hot Californian sun like bacilli in a test-tube.

Next to Snyder sat his attorney, Porter Dillon, a sharply-dressed, fresh-faced young man with abundant shoulder-length hair, who enjoyed the reputation of being a 'radical lawyer'. He was busy taking notes, when Ann Kelsey rose to her feet, addressing Judge Olga Winbush.

'Your Honour, before you bring in the jury, I'd like to renew my Motion for Severance.'

The judge frowned. 'On what grounds?'

'On the grounds that the presence of this co-defendant' – Ann gestured towards Russ Snyder – 'will result in a confusion of the issues and materially prejudice my client's right to a fair trial.'

Snyder let out a low chortle of derision. 'What's the matter – doesn't your client like my smell?' he cooed, in a surprisingly soft, beguiling voice directed at Eugene Etter, who was sitting stolidly beside Ann Kelsey.

The President of Humbolt Logging flushed with anger, but sat tight, pretending to ignore him.

Porter Dillon was now on his feet. 'Your Honour,' he said silkily, 'we share counsel's concern that Humbolt Logging's impeccable reputation for the rape and pillage of the redwoods could be sullied by association with my client, who is a concerned environmentalist . . .'

Ann Kelsey broke in haughtily: 'Your Honour, this is just the kind of mud-slinging I anticipate.'

Russ Snyder sat back, grinning through his matted whiskers; he was already enjoying himself hugely.

'Mr Dillon,' Judge Olga Winbush snapped, 'why are you on your feet in the middle of Ms Kelsey's motion?'

'Because I agree with her!' the young attorney said,

entirely unfazed. 'My client shouldn't be here – now or later. I renew my motion to dismiss the case against Mr Snyder. There is no evidence to suggest . . .'

'Let's hear the evidence, Mr Dillon,' Judge Winbush said impatiently. 'Motion denied.' She turned to Ann Kelsey. 'As to your motion' – she indicated a compact, tough-looking man built like a small tank, sitting at a separate table in the court – '*this* gentleman claims that your client and Mr Dillon's client both shared in the acts that led to his injury.'

The 'gentleman' she was referring to was the plaintiff, Wayne Paul. He too had a beard and was roughly-dressed, but there were two marked differences between him and Russ Snyder. Wayne Paul had worked all his life out of doors, and he only had one arm.

The judge continued: 'I don't think finger-pointing *will* confuse the jury, Ms Kelsey. Blame is the sole issue. Motion denied.'

Ann Kelsey sat down, masking her disappointment. Beside her, Russ Dillon murmured, 'Tough break,' in a low insinuating voice. She ignored him.

*

The face on the hospital pillow was an abject sight. Douglas Brackman's cheeks were swollen, his eyes puffed and purple, his nose encased in a broad white swathe of bandage. Leland McKenzie sat gingerly beside him on the edge of the counterpane.

'What did your doctor advise?' he asked anxiously.

'I advised *him*,' Brackman said, in a thick voice full of depressed discomfort. 'Advised him that I'm receiving a

118

major award from the Bar Association and that it would take more than a random act of urban violence to prevent me from attending.'

Leland looked gravely down at his partner, concerned and worried. 'Douglas – I just talked to Detective Connolly out in the hall . . .'

'And?' Brackman's swollen eyes did not permit him to express any worry in return.

'He explained to me about the' – McKenzie gave a short cough – 'about the exact nature of the establishment you'd been visiting.'

'It's not an establishment,' said Brackman. 'It's a restaurant.'

'That's entirely your business.' The Senior Partner's voice had taken on a slight edge. 'And as far as I'm concerned, it'll stay that way.'

Douglas Brackman shifted uncomfortably on the bed. 'Are you . . .?' – he tried to raise his head from the pillow – 'for goodness sake, Leland! – I was meeting an old friend there!'

'You don't have to explain your friendships, Douglas. I've never meddled in the private affairs of colleagues.'

'It was *not* a private affair!' Brackman said, and this time his swollen eyes showed slits of anger.

'Douglas, you're a damned fine lawyer,' McKenzie said elliptically, 'and that's all that matters to me.'

This time Brackman managed to haul his head off the pillow. 'Leland –!' he began, just as the door opened and a chunky grey man came in, unsmiling, carrying a battered briefcase. As he closed the door, Brackman made a weak gesture towards his Senior Partner: 'Mr Leland McKenzie – Detective Connolly . . .' – forgetting that the two had already met outside. The detective nodded. 'Excuse me, gentlemen. Feeling better, Mr Brackman?'

'No.'

Connolly gave what passed for a smile. 'Well, I got something that's gonna make us both feel better. I've been after this S.O.B. for months now.'

'What are you doing about him?' asked Brackman.

'Photo gallery. We've picked up a suspect we'd like you to I.D. And I've got three others like you I'd like you to talk to.'

'*Like me?*' Brackman repeated, with deep suspicion.

'Other victims of this gay-bashing nut,' the detective said evenly.

'I resent the implication.' Brackman managed to sound pompous, even through his injuries.

'You got a look at him,' the detective went on. 'That ought to give us a line on him.'

'I want no part of this,' Brackman said.

'Come on, Douglas,' said McKenzie, as the detective started leafing through a folder in his case.

'Get those photos out of here! I'm not pressing charges.' Brackman's head had slid back on to the pillow, his puffed eyes staring deliberately at the wall. The detective and the Senior Partner exchanged a brief glance.

*

Attorney James Pavlik was a prim, balding little man, about half the size of his client, the bearded plaintiff Wayne Paul, who now stood on the witness stand with the sleeve of his missing arm turned slightly toward the jury.

He was telling Pavlik and the court: 'Next thing I knew,

I was on the deck. Metal had stopped flying and the rig operator was kneeling on my arm, trying to stop the bleeding.'

'Was it customary for you to be so close to the blades?' his attorney, Pavlik, asked.

'Yessir! As off-bearer in the sawmill, it was my job to reach with a pike and guide the slabs.' He made a complicated, sideways movement from the hips, swinging his whole weight behind his good arm.

'And that's how you guided the logs?'

'Not exactly,' Wayne Paul said. 'I used my right arm.'

Pavlik lowered his head, allowing the answer to register fully with the jury. 'Thank you,' he said. 'Nothing further.'

*

Ann Kelsey rose. 'Mr Paul, is it unusual for a band-saw to strike foreign objects embedded in logs?'

The big man shrugged. 'Blades don't break every day, ma'am.'

'But in your experience? I mean, you've had blades strike nails from old homesteads, for example?'

'Yes, ma'am.'

'And ceramic insulators from telephone lines?'

'Yes.'

'And hunters' bullets, and stones and horseshoes, and even cable from your own millpond?'

Wayne Paul gave another shrug. 'This time it hit a spike.'

Ann Kelsey paused. 'Mr Paul, didn't you originally turn down the job as off-bearer at South Creek?'

'Yeah,' said Wayne Paul. 'I'd been head rig-operator at Ukiah, and off-bearer was a step down.'

121

'What made it a "step down".'

'Less money.' The man grinned. 'And harder work.'

'And more dangerous?' Ann Kelsey asked. There was a pause. 'Come on,' she said. 'Anyone in a mill knows that off-bearer is the highest risk . . .'

'Objection,' said Pavlik. 'Calls for speculation.'

'Sustained,' said Judge Olga Winbush.

'Is it true,' Ann Kelsey continued, 'that you were cited for marijuana use on the job . . .'

Pavlik leapt up. 'Objection! Immaterial!'

'That was fifteen years ago,' Paul said, getting angry.

Ann Kelsey added quickly, 'The plaintiff's comparative negligence is relevant here.'

'Your Honour,' said Porter Dillon smoothly, rising to his feet, 'this is typical of the industry's callow disregard for its own workers. I ask, therefore, that the record show that the co-defence in this case does not share in this irrelevant accusation.'

'Sit down, Mr Dillon,' the judge said brutally.

The fresh-faced young attorney looked surprised, but as he resumed his seat, the burly figure of Russ Snyder lean out along the defendant's table and called out, in a husky whisper. 'Keep at it, Etter! He's still got two legs!'

'Mr Dillon, control your client!' snapped Judge Win bush, 'or I'll cite him in contempt. The objection i sustained, Ms Kelsey,' she added – although by now most o the court, including the jury, could have been forgiven fo having forgotten what the original objection was against.

Ann continued: 'Mr Paul, were you drinking at the "Blu Ox Tavern" until three a.m. on the morning of th accident?'

'That blade did *not* break,' the one-armed man said

'because I drank a sixer! It broke because that big jackass along there drove a six-inch spike into the meat of the tree, and Mr Etter there didn't do jack about it!'

'Move to strike!' said Ann Kelsey.

'The jury will disregard that outburst,' Judge Winbush said.

'Did you leave the "Blue Ox" only four hours before your shift began on the day of your accident?' Ann went on.

'Yeah,' Wayne Paul growled.

'Thank you. Nothing further.'

'Your Honour,' Porter Dillon said ingratiatingly, 'we have no questions for Mr Paul.'

The judge adjourned until next morning.

'Nice stunt, Counsellor,' Ann said calmly to Porter Dillon, and began collecting her papers from the table.

'Stunt?' the fresh-faced man replied, beginning to frown.

'Your shock over my mention of marijuana. You know darned well, if I hadn't brought it up, you would have.'

'Maybe,' Porter Dillon said, with a sly smile. 'But you saved me the trouble. I won't have to roll up my sleeves until we get to the good part!'

Ann finished gathering together her papers. She decided she didn't much like young Porter Dillon.

Chapter Thirteen

Douglas Brackman stood resplendent in black tie, pumping hands under the marble and mahogany splendour of the Los Angeles Bar Association's banqueting hall. The dinner had been magnificent; the speeches uplifting – his own, he was assured, the best of all. His triumph seemed complete.

His appearance, too, had not been so bad. The bandaging was reduced to a thin strip of white that might have been mistaken by those at the back of the hall for a shine on his prominent nose; and his dark eyes, deep-set under their heavy brows, had been further offset by shadow from the overhead lighting so that the puffed bruising hardly showed until seen close up.

The worst part was his cracked rib. It hurt like hell every time he moved, and was pure agony when he laughed or coughed, so that his naturally humourless demeanour was even more rigid and gloomy than usual. Towards the end of the dinner, the tight strapping under his shirt had begun to itch and pulsate; and towards the end of the meal he'd been half-writhing in his seat, scarcely able to control a compulsive urge to scratch.

Now, with the freedom to move, he felt some relief, but

the strain was beginning to tell. He was exhausted and slightly muzzy from painkillers, his domed forehead glistening with sweat, his throat growing hoarse and sore, and his hand trembling after a single coffee. (He'd kept strictly off liquor all evening on account of the medication.)

He stood now at the vaulted entrance to the banqueting hall, still holding the bronze plaque he'd been awarded, tucked awkwardly under his arm, shaking hands with his free hand. His smile was forced but genuine. The plaudits and congratulations were falling fast, as the guests streamed out.

In his acceptance speech he'd been witty, avuncular, modest, and above all, brief. He'd mentioned his dead father four times and his mother twice, had spoken of himself when a child of six, of his early desire to be a cowboy, of how his dead mother had asked him why he wanted to be a cowboy, and how he'd announced, '*So I can get the bad guys!*' That had gone down real well, and after that he'd had his illustrious audience eating out of his hand. He'd told them how his father had then said to him – and he could remember the words as though it were yesterday: 'Looks like we have one more attorney in the family – *another Brackman interested in Justice!*' The applause had been so loud and sustained that for a couple of minutes he'd even forgotten the pain in his ribs.

Brackman had made a final joke about not knowing if he'd feel as honoured today if he were being honoured as Downtown Los Angeles Cowboy-of-the-Month, and had again basked in the cheering and applause; and had signed off with an authentic catch-in-the-throat, as he said, 'I only hope my father hears and knows he shares in this great honour . . .'

125

The last guests were now passing him. A retired Supreme Court judge, stooped and frail, paused and clutched his hand. 'Fine speech, Brackman! The American Bar is proud of you.' Brackman's heart swelled under the tight bandaging, but his delight was short-lived. Behind the old judge, among the final half-dozen guests, he saw Robert Caporale approaching.

The fixed smile died on Brackman's lips. His heart now began to beat painfully, as Caporale came level with him. 'Great speech, Douglas!'

Brackman lowered his voice, muttering, 'Sorry I haven't answered any of your calls . . .'

Caporale moved closer, so that Brackman could smell his aftershave: 'I feel responsible,' he said softly.

Brackman stiffened, glancing at the last two guests in the line. 'You shouldn't,' he said quickly. 'It was a random event.'

'But it wasn't,' the other persisted. 'What happened to you happens to thousands of gay men and women every year.'

For God's sake! Brackman thought, and shook hands with the last two well-wishers, watching with relief as they moved out of earshot. 'Anyway, this particular thug's been apprehended,' he said.

Caporale stood shaking his head. 'The police case is falling apart. No-one can make a positive I.D.'

'That's unfortunate,' Brackman said. His head was throbbing and he suddenly, desperately wanted to get away from here – take some more painkillers and go to bed.

Caporale looked at him severely, accusingly. 'Yeah. For a moment, Douglas, it looked like we were gonna get those "bad guys".' There was a slow-burning anger in his voice now. 'Nice speech, Douglas,' he added bitterly, turning to go.

Against his better judgement, Brackman stopped him. In a hushed voice, still terrified they'd be overheard, he said to his old friend, 'Bob, how can you – of all people – expect me to get involved in this? You've kept silent yourself for years because you knew the rumour of homosexuality could hurt you professionally – could even *ruin* you . . .'

'That's just why I'm starting to speak out. I know how damaging silence and secrecy can be!' Caporale turned and began striding away. Brackman winced. He was covered in sweat and the pain was excruciating.

*

There were four of them in the witness room of the Civil Court. It was stuffy and tempers were frayed. Ann Kelsey had summoned the meeting with Porter Dillon and his client, Russ Snyder. She was sitting with her own client, Eugene Etter, of Humbolt Logging. Only the eager-beaver, Porter Dillon, looked friendly, and that was deceptive.

It was make-or-break, Ann knew, and dreaded it. Even with her experience as an attorney, she was never really happy with the confrontational side of the law. In a courtroom it was all right – there were strict rules and conventions, and a good judge to sit as referee. But when it came down to basic, hostile personalities, she found it a nightmare.

Porter Dillon, on the other hand, seemed to have no such reservations. He grinned at her and said brashly, 'What's on your mind, lady?'

Ann ignored the gross familiarity. 'I think the longer this

goes on, the bigger the money's going to get. Why don't we try to come up with a number, split it fifty-fifty, and offer to settle?'

The young attorney thought for a moment, then nodded. 'I think you're right – we ought to settle. What's more, I think my client's fair share' – he glanced at Russ Snyder beside him – 'should be a big Zero. Not one dime.'

The boss of Humbolt Logging lumbered to his feet. 'Let's get out of here . . .' Etter began.

'My client did not spike that tree,' Dillon said.

Eugene Etter swung round, his big hands balled into fists at his side. 'The hell he didn't!' he growled.

Ann looked quickly at her client. 'Mr Etter –' she began, when Russ Snyder, lounging back in his seat, sneered up at the boss of the logging company.

'How would you know, Etter, what goes on in the woods? You spend your whole time in the office counting your money!'

Etter took a step forward. 'Your rich son-of-a . . .! You trying to tell me about *money*! I hunted and fished those woods my whole goddam life while you were being pampered by your rich daddy . . . out playing with your nanny . . .!' The man stood shaking with rage.

Russ smiled and said, in his soft city-bred voice: 'And where the hell do you think *your* kids are going to be able to take *their* kids to hunt and fish?'

Porter Dillon broke in, 'There's more at stake here than who pays what. A way of life is being threatened.'

'On both sides,' Ann said. 'And if we can't help these two men find some common ground – well, then I fear there'll be more violence. And more victims like Wayne Paul.'

'That's fine with them,' Etter snarled. '"Long as no *trees* get hurt ... they don't give a darn about workers losing jobs!'

Snyder roused his shaggy head. '*Over-harvesting* – that's what's killing the industry!'

Eugene Etter suddenly slammed a fist on the table. 'Listen, you great creep! People want *wood*!' – and he began thumping the solid oak surface – 'People want *paper*!' – scooping up a handful of documents off the table.

'Sure – people in Japan,' Snyder grinned. 'That's your big market these days – *right*?'

'You sonofabitch1' Etter started to move round the table, his hands ready to tear Snyder's limbs off his big body. Porter Dillon stepped nimbly between them. 'Now, now, boys!' he said, with surprising cool.

Ann stood up, ashen-faced. Dillon looked at her and chuckled: 'I think we can forget the settlement,' he said, but he didn't sound disappointed. If these two apes wanted to fight it out, it was more money in the bank for Porter Dillon.

*

The President of Humbolt Logging had barely had time to cool off. He now stood, in his awkward city-suit, moustache bristling, facing his attorney from the witness stand.

Ann Kelsey asked him, 'And when you received the warning, Mr Etter, how did you respond?'

'I sent a team out to see if it was true.'

'Did you have reason to suspect the warning wasn't true?'

'I'd gotten two earlier ones on other tracts, but we never found any spikes.'

'Why would they warn of spikes – if they hadn't actually spiked the trees?'

Etter sighed. 'You gotta understand these so-called "Redwood Warriors". Their whole mission in life is to put loggers out of business. They'll do anything to cost me time and money.'

'Such as?' asked Ann.

'Such as damage vehicles and equipment; chaining themselves up in trees. They're up to every trick in the book!'

'On this occasion, did your team find any evidence of spiking?'

'No,' said Etter. 'They didn't find anything.'

'Did you take any other action?'

'Well' – Etter paused – 'I called up Russ Snyder personally and cussed him out – *personally*.'

'Why?'

'He's their ringleader. Ask anyone in town!'

'Objection,' said Porter Dillon. 'Hearsay.'

'Sustained.'

'And what was Russ Snyder's reaction to your call?' asked Ann.

'He laughed at me.'

'Did he deny responsibility for the spiking?'

'No – he sure didn't!'

Ann Kelsey thanked her client and sat down. James Pavlik, the attorney for the one-armed defendant, Wayne Paul, now rose. He was a short, fussy little man; his manner brisk and business-like.

'Mr Etter, what was your team doing as they walked the tract?'

'Looking for spikes,' Etter said grimly.

'They were eye-balling?'

'That's right.'

'But didn't they know that tree-spikers snip the heads off the nails so they can't be detected?'

'Yeah – that's why they also had metal detectors.'

'But aren't ceramic spikes also used?'

'Sure! Sometimes they drill holes and pour in rocks or cement. You can't out-guess these nuts.'

'No,' said Pavlik. 'You can't indeed out-guess these nuts. But you still took only minor precautions . . .'

'I did all I could!' Etter roared.

Pavlik nodded calmly. 'Approximately how many trees are on an acre of old-growth trees, Mr Etter?'

'It varies. Three hundred, maybe.'

'So your team ran a metal detector over twelve thousand trees – is that right?'

'No – they used it on a sampling.'

'Oh? On what then? Half the trees? Six thousand?'

'It's hard to say.' Etter was frowning; he sounded worried.

'More than a hundred?' said Pavlik. He smiled. 'You see, Mr Etter, I'm trying to get a feel for what makes up a sampling.'

'Maybe a few hundred,' Etter said.

'A few hundred – out of twelve thousand?' Pavlik was still smiling. He paused. 'Mr Etter, after you logged this tract, did you alert the sawmill about the possibility of spikes?'

'No – I didn't think it was necessary.'

Pavlik nodded again. 'But you were wrong about that – weren't you?'

'I did my best,' Etter muttered.

'Were you wrong?'

The big man sighed. 'Yeah, I guess so.'

'Nothing further,' said Pavlik, and sat down.

*

It was now Porter Dillon's turn to face the boss of Humbolt Logging. He shook his shoulder-length hair, fiddled with his brightly-coloured tie, then gave Eugene Etter a long, appraising look, like a zoologist inspecting some dangerous but near-extinct predatory beast.

'Mr Etter,' Dillon began, 'what method of forestry did you use to harvest the Salt Fork Tract?'

'We clear cut it.'

'Meaning you went through and levelled every two thousand year old tree?'

'And replanted,' Etter said firmly, 'as mandated by the Forest Service.'

'How's the replanting going?' Dillon asked casually. Behind him his client, Wayne Paul, listened keenly, his empty sleeve tucked up under the fold of his rough jacket.

'What d'you mean?' Etter said.

'How's the re-seeded forest look today?'

Etter hesitated. 'I haven't seen it recently.'

'So you haven't seen where mudslides washed away your re-seeding, along with three feet of topsoil?'

Ann Kelsey was on her feet. 'Objection! Relevance! Is my client now responsible for flash-floods?'

'Sustained,' said Judge Olga Winbush, just as Russ Snyder called out: 'He didn't leave anything to hold the soil – *that's why*, the dumb bastard!'

'You're out of order, Mr Snyder!' the judge warned.

132

Porter Dillon looked across at Ann. 'Your client is responsible for deciding to cut that timber, come hell or high water.'

'That's enough,' said Judge Winbush. 'Move on.'

Dillon turned again to the stand. 'Why were you in such a rush to harvest this old growth, Mr Etter?'

'Objection,' interrupted Ann Kelsey.

Dillon deferred to her, with a faint smile. 'I'll rephrase that. Isn't it true, Mr Etter, that you were racing to beat a court injunction to preserve that stand?'

'We're always racing,' Etter said; he sounded weary now. 'We loggers have *given and given*. We lose the old growth, then they start hollering about water quality and wetlands and habitat, and the whole damned works! They're never satisfied. They don't *want* to be satisfied. All I do is supply a public demand – and put food on my family's table.' He glared down at Russ Snyder, who smirked back.

'And how much public demand was there,' Dillon went on, 'for the tree that was being milled when Mr Paul was injured? How much did that particular tree bring?'

'Twenty thousand dollars,' Etter said quietly.

'*Twenty-thousand dollars for one tree?*' Porter Dillon exclaimed, with mock incredulity. 'That ought to put a few meals on the table for you, Mr Etter!'

'Objection!' cried Ann.

'Withdrawn. Nothing further,' said Dillon. He smiled and sat down.

*

Douglas Brackman was back in his office next day. He sat in the easy chair, his hands in his lap, and stared out of the window. The sky was clear and the desk beside him was neat and tidy. Perhaps too tidy.

He was very pale; there was still a small bandage on his nose, but the bruising was now no more than dark smudges round his eyes. He heard a gentle knock, and someone came in. It was Roxanne. 'Here are your Spiedel contracts,' she said, hesitating at the door.

Brackman didn't move, didn't look at her. 'Leave them on my desk,' he said quietly.

She stepped up beside him, put the papers down, and said, 'Maybe you should go home early. Don't push it on your first day back.'

Brackman was still staring out of the window. He spoke without moving his head: 'Ever ridden a horse, Roxanne?'

'Oh, when I was a girl I loved to ride!'

'The horses didn't frighten you?'

'No . . .' she said doubtfully.

'I wanted to be a cowboy once – until I was six,' he said. He was half-talking to himself. 'Then my mother took me one day to a stable near Griffith Park. The horses there were huge. They hadn't ever looked that big in the movies. I wouldn't go near them – let alone get on one. And in one crushing instant I knew I was too scared to be a cowboy.' He turned. 'I was a coward, Roxanne.' He sat nodding for a moment, while she just stood looking at him. Then he gave a little shrug. 'Fortunately my father had other plans for me.'

Roxanne took a deep breath. She felt confused, even embarrassed. 'Well,' she said, trying to sound cheerful. 'I certainly think you make a better attorney than you would ever have made a cowboy! But I don't think you're a coward,' she added bravely. When he didn't reply, she took a step forward. 'Are you still afraid of horses?'

'I avoid horses.' He was looking out of the window again.

Roxanne paused. She looked puzzled, perhaps a little worried. This wasn't her old dour and decisive Brackman – far from it! And for a moment she wondered if he might have suffered some mild brain damage in his accident. *Oh God*, she thought, and after a moment, quietly withdrew.

She considered whether she ought to mention the incident to Leland? She began to be seriously worried about Douglas. It had quite made her forget that Arnie had hardly spoken a word to her for twenty-four hours.

Chapter Fourteen

Arnie Becker hurried in late for Morning Conference. 'Sorry – I had a six a.m. photo shoot.' He grinned defensively round the table, and noticed, with relief tinged with guilt, that Roxanne wasn't present. He was conscious that he'd been rather neglecting her recently – but then, what could he do? Being a T.V. star left one so little free time . . .

'The Station has me on a brutal P.R. schedule!' he added, taking his seat. Most of the table, except Leland McKenzie, let out a burst of ironic applause. Susan Bloom smiled indulgently at her newest protegé, while Douglas Brackman, chairing his first conference since returning to work, preferred to remain silent on the subject of Arnie's second 'career' – which he knew was directly down to Bloom, and therefore indirectly to him.

He consulted the agenda again. 'Right. Next up – Kendrick versus McArthur.' He glanced at Bloom. 'You're taking this?'

'That's right, Dougie.' – (Brackman winced visibly) – 'We oversized people have to stick together! It's a matter of solidarity,' she added, smiling voraciously round the table.

'This is the case of the man who was assaulted in a health food shake?' asked Ann.

'Gives the term "food-fight" a whole new meaning,' Castroverti chuckled.

'It was a diet shake,' Bloom said importantly. 'This case is all about *weight*. I'm an expert on the subject and I figure to wipe out the opposition on this one.'

Brackman frowned suddenly. 'But Susan . . .?'

'Yeah?'

'I mean, isn't the fat guy' – he checked himself, cleared his throat – 'I mean, the oversized party – isn't *he* the opposition? Aren't you for the plaintiff?'

'Sure.' Bloom beamed at him. 'Doesn't mean I have to be always *for* these oversized people. We're individuals, too, you know! Just that I'm an expert, like I said. I know the psychology.'

'*Psychology*?' Brackman was visibly puzzled.

'Yeah, I understand what makes fat people tick. We don't all have to be saints, y'know.'

'I know.'

'Besides,' she added breezily, 'it proves I'm impartial!'

'Yes.' Brackman nodded, po-faced. 'Kendrick versus McArthur. So it's all yours, Susan. Good luck.'

*

It was one of those court scenes that all judges hate. The line-up in Civil Court Number Two looked this morning more like the scene for a vaudeville act than a sober court of justice. But, as on all such occasions, the majesty of the Law had to command total solemnity. Laughter, even smiles, were not to be tolerated. Judge Walter Swanson, known to be a severe man, would make sure of that.

Susan Bloom had the plaintiff – a puny, mean-faced little man called Lyle Kendrick, one-time restaurateur and now owner of a health food establishment in downtown L.A. – up on the stand. Beside her, at the defendant's table, sat a spectacularly fat man.

Corliss McArthur must have weighed over two hundred and fifty pounds; and the casual observer could not help wondering how the standard-issue courtroom chair could bear his weight. The man's thighs and buttocks, in their outsize trousers, bulged like cloth-wrapped hams over the sides of the chair and his great pink hands lay on the table in front of him like a pair of prime baby pigs ripe for the butcher's slab.

Bloom said to the puny man on the stand, 'You've had your concession on Hollywood Boulevard for how long Mr Kendrick?'

'Twenty-five years,' he said proudly. 'I'm a Hollywood fixture – ask anybody!'

'And Mr McArthur here has been patronising you for the past two of these years?'

'Yeah. He'd come over every day, order a Health Shake, sometimes a veggieburger. We'd talk sports – all very cordial. That's why it was such a shock.'

'The assault?' said Bloom.

'Yeah. I mean, one minute I'm ringing up a sale, the next *he's* bearing down on me' – he nodded at Corliss McArthur, who sat chewing a thumb the size of a king prawn – 'I tell you, the floor's shaking with every step, like I thought I was in the buffalo stampede from *Dances with Wolves*!'

The man's attorney, Joe Dumphy, broke in: 'Objection to the buffalo characterisation, Your Honour.'

'Sustained,' said Judge Swanson.

'And what did McArthur do next?' asked Bloom.

'Started yelling at me. Yelling and cursing – calling me a fraud and a liar. He was blaming *me* for *his* gaining weight! It was crazy – he was totally out of control! He started demanding an apology – demanding his money back . . .!'

'And then?'

'Well,' said Kendrick, 'I turned to walk away, and he reached out and grabbed me. He pushed me down, and then' – he gave a little shudder at the memory – '*he sat on me*!'

Judge Swanson leaned forward, looking puzzled. 'Excuse me?'

'He *sat* on me,' Kendrick repeated. 'And he wouldn't get up! Then I heard a crack. It was a ballpoint pen in my pocket – and they had to surgically remove the ink cartridge from my thigh!'

'How long did Mr McArthur keep you forcibly restrained?' Bloom asked.

'About five minutes, I guess. Until the police showed up.'

'And what injuries did you suffer as a result of this unprovoked attack?'

'A herniated disc – I may need an operation. I can only stand for an hour, and it's killing my business. And all because of *him*.' He shot an outraged look at the fat man who went on calmly chewing his thumb.

'Thank you, Mr Kendrick. No more questions.'

Joe Dumphy now rose, holding out a promotional flysheet in his hand. 'Mr Kendrick, your ads say you offer

– and I quote – '*Fast Food That Isn't Fast Fat*'. Low-calorie, nutritious snacks and shakes. Right?'

'Yeah – and I never had a dissatisfied customer yet, till Babar the Elephant over there!'

'Move to strike Babar the Elephant,' said Dumphy.

'So ordered,' said the judge, with the utmost seriousness.

'And you claim your Health Shake is low-calorie?' Dumphy went on.

'Absolutely,' said Kendrick. 'Water, soya-paste, skimmed milk. Seventy calories only.'

'But what you *don't* advertise,' said Dumphy, ' is the calorie content of the *flavourings* that you put *into* this alleged "Health Shake".'

He began to read from a list of ingredients: 'Pineapple, guava, and papaya juice – *all at a hundred calories apiece*. And banana puree – *one hundred and sixty-eight* calories! So instead of *seventy* calories, your basic "Health Shake" actually contains *six-hundred and seventy* calories – isn't that correct?'

Kendrick swung his short arms in protest. 'Hey, he didn't *have* to order the flavourings?'

'Ah c'mon, sir,' Dumphy said, 'we both know the plain stuff tastes like coolant fluid.'

'Objection!' cried Susan Bloom.

'Sustained.'

Joe Dumphy continued: 'Fact is, Mr Kendrick, no-one would *drink* your so-called "Health Shake" if it didn't have the flavourings – now would they?'

'That's absolutely not true! *Lots* of my customers drink the plain shake. I drink it myself . . .!'

'Oh, really?' said Dumphy; he turned, as a man moved out from the back of the courtroom, carrying a tray with a

140

dozen cartons marked '*Hendrick Health Shakes – the Slimmest for the Trimmest.*' Dumphy waited until they were placed on the defendant's table, then addressed the judge:

'Your Honour, the parties stipulate that these are Mr Kendrick's basic seventy calorie shakes. I'd like the jury to sample them.'

'Your Honour,' Susan Bloom interrupted, 'I renew my objection to this. Each juror's palate is different. This experiment is therefore highly subjective and totally . . .'

'Overruled,' snapped Judge Swanson. 'But get on with it, Mr Dumphy.'

The assistant began carefully to hand out the twelve cartons, each with a straw supplied. None of the jurors looked entirely happy with the experiment, even less so when they began to suck in the contents. One of them, an elderly man with a hearing-aid, looked ready to spit it out, glanced desperately round, sucked in his cheeks and finally swallowed the stuff, before sitting back looking as sick as a parrot.

Judge Swanson's face remained admirably straight. 'Let the record show,' he said drily, 'that none of the jurors turned somersaults of joy on sampling the evidence.'

Joe Dumphy turned back to the witness, waving a hand in the direction of the stricken jurors. 'So as we've just seen, Mr Kendrick – your basic shake is undrinkable. And to get customers like Mr McArthur to drink it, you had to soft-sell them on flavourings that made them gain weight. And Mr McArthur *did* most surely gain weight.' He nodded at the fat man, who was now greedily munching the heel of his hand.

'Nobody held a gun to his head and *made* him drink it,' Hendrick said plaintively.

'No,' said Dumphy, 'you didn't have to. You just start him off with one, talk batting averages, then slide him another one before rounding off the Top Ten. Home-runs. RBI's – '*Here, Mr McArthur, have another – try the raspberry this time!*' You had him drinking five or six a day, didn't you?'

Kendrick was going red in the face. 'That doesn't give him the right to attack me!'

'Didn't you call him a "fat-ass pig"?'

'Yeah!' Kendrick cried. 'After *he* called *me* a liar! And then he assaults me with a deadly weapon!'

'I don't think,' Dumphy said, 'the State of California classifies a *derrière* as a deadly weapon . . .?'

'Well, *his* sure as hell is!' Kendrick yelled.

'It was your shakes that were deadly, sir,' Dumphy said portentously. 'And you kept pumping them into poor Corliss McArthur here. You just kept up those sales, so you could make more money!'

'Objection!' said Bloom.

'Withdrawn,' said Dumphy. 'I'm done here.' And he sat down beside his client, who just went on gnawing bits of his hand.

*

'Mr Snyder, as leader of the "Redwood Warriors", haven' you given numerous speeches advocating tree-spiking? Ann Kelsey kept the bearded, soft-spoken man in her sights, not forgetting for a moment that she had a 'brief' to stick to: that her personal opinions must in no way bend her judgement. Emotionally, all her sympathies were with the threatened redwoods. On the other hand, the boss o

Humbolt Logging was paying her fees; and above all, she had a duty to her client. She'd also decided that she found her adversary, Russ Snyder, an odiously sanctimonious, well-bred young ruffian – just the type, she reasoned, to give the whole environmental lobby a bad name.

'I never advocated violence,' Snyder now answered her, in a tone of soft menace.

'But you understood the danger?' she said. 'That's the whole point of using spikes – right?'

'No. The point was to act as a deterrent. That's why I always stressed marking trees and sending warnings.'

'You thought six-inch spikes of galvanised steel could be driven into logs that were headed for saw-blades moving eight thousand board-feet a minute, *without the risk of a worker being injured*?'

'I thought the presence of spikes would prevent giant sequoias from being milled,' he answered, completely calm.

'But you were mistaken.'

'The only mistake I made was over-estimating the logging company's concern for their workers' safety.'

'A man was severely injured by one of your spikes,' Ann said flatly.

'Objection!' cried Porter Dillon: 'Not a shred of evidence has been produced that links this spike to my client.'

'Sustained,' said Judge Winbush.

'Mr Snyder,' Ann went on, 'what is the motto which you wrote for the "Redwood Warriors"?'

'"Equal Rights for Mother Earth".'

'And what does that mean?'

'It means,' Snyder said, leaning forward slightly, and making to address the whole courtroom, 'that the natural world doesn't exist solely for human beings to exploit. All forms of life on this Earth have an inherent value.'

'But "*equal*" value?' Ann persisted. 'The loss of a tree, for example, is worth the loss of a man's arm?'

'That's not a fair comparison,' he said, with deprecating self-righteousness.

Ann nodded energetically. 'I agree, Mr Snyder! It's not fair. Not fair at all! Nothing further.'

Her place was taken by Pavlik. 'Mr Snyder, weren't you twice discovered trespassing on the Salt Fork tract?'

'I was seen taking a walk in the woods,' he said smugly.

'And on the first day of tree harvesting, were you arrested for chaining yourself to a crawler-tractor at the site?'

Snyder gave a low chuckle. 'Sure! That's why I couldn't have spiked anything. I was all tied up!'

'Move to strike,' Pavlik said to the judge.

'So moved. The jury will disregard. Stick to answering the questions asked, Mr Snyder.'

Snyder gave a contemptuous shrug.

'At the time of your arrest,' said Pavlik, 'did the police confiscate from you a box of nails?'

'Yeah – from the toolbox in my truck!' he cried. 'I'm a carpenter, for Chrissake!'

Pavlik nodded. 'Nothing more for now.'

It was Porter Dillon's turn. He turned solemnly to his client. 'Mr Snyder, are you indeed a spokesman for the "Redwood Warriors"?'

'And proud of it!' he answered.

'Were you always an environmental radical?'

'Objection!' said Ann Kelsey. 'The evolution of this man's philosophy is not relevant.'

'I'll allow the question,' Judge Winbush said.

'After ten years in the environmental movement,' Russ Snyder replied, 'I realised nothing's changed. We're still devastating old-growth trees at the unchecked rate of seventy thousand acres a year. At that rate, there will be no virgin woods left in this State in twenty years!'

Peter Dillon nodded. 'Certainly we all like trees, Mr Snyder. But aren't your tactics extreme?'

Snyder's reply was well-rehearsed and word-perfect: 'This isn't just about the beauty of primal forests!' he declaimed. 'It's about our very survival on this planet. These old-growth eco-systems clean the air – they protect the watershed. Yes – our antics may seem extreme, but the systematic annihilation of our environment wasn't fazed by any less extreme actions.'

'Objection,' said Ann. 'This isn't an answer – it's a prepared sermon.'

'Sustained.'

'One more question,' said Porter Dillon. 'Do you believe that any means justify the end in protecting these ancient forests?'

'No,' Snyder said firmly. 'But as citizens, the wilderness is part of our home. And just like you'd defend your home if someone broke in, so I want to protect these woods. But I advocate only non-violent tactics.'

'Thank you.'

*

The leader of the 'Redwood Warriors' was about to leave the witness stand, when Ann Kelsey said, 'One further question, Mr Snyder. Would you describe Mr Wayne Paul's injury as non-violent?'

'No. I would not.'

'Nothing further. We rest, Your Honour.'

As she resumed her seat, Porter Dillon rose. 'In that case, Your Honour, I move for a directed verdict. The plaintiff and co-defence have failed to present a *prima facie* case against my client, Mr Snyder.'

There was a burst of hopeful applause from the spectators' gallery, followed by a loud murmur of discussion. The atmosphere in the courtroom became very tense. Ann Kelsey was now standing:

'Your Honour, Mr Dillon's client *admits* to spiking the trees. He was seen on the property!'

There were boos from the gallery, and some sporadic cheering. Judge Olga Winbush glanced up, frowning, then leant forward and said, 'I'm sorry, Ms Kelsey. But I agree with Mr Dillon.'

Ann was defiant. 'If you dismiss this co-defendant, Your Honour, you're removing the party who maliciously and criminally began the chain of events that led directly to this action!'

The judge sighed and leaned on her elbows, addressing the whole court: 'As much as I would like to have the party who spiked this tree held liable for his, or her, actions, this court has not heard any evidence that could reasonably link this defendant to this spiking. According, I direct that Mr Snyder be dismissed from this law suit.'

There was loud applause at this, and Russ Snyder left the witness stand giving the two-handed boxers' victory salute. Porter Dillon was wearing his familiar smirk, while Ann Kelsey slowly sat down, disappointed, even worried.

'Adjourned for one hour,' said Judge Winbush.

In the witness room a few minutes later, Ann Kelsey was locked in a furious argument with her client, Eugene Etter. The burly head of Humbolt Logging was almost shouting at her: 'I thought we *wanted* them out of the case!'

'I wanted the case severed,' she said. 'I didn't want the brute walking away free! Now the jury's heard him, there's nothing we can do to recall him.'

'And I come off as the bad guy?' Etter snarled.

'They see an injured victim, Mr Etter.' She was trying to stay cool. 'They see animosity between the two of you.'

'So those bastards break the law and I pay the bill! *That* it?'

'We can settle without admitting negligence,' she said quietly.

'So they got to you, too, did they?' He stood shaking his head in enraged disbelief. 'Those goddam spikers – those *terrorists* – have got you thinking it's all my fault!'

'Mr Etter' – Ann's voice was still steady – 'I'm making a professional recommendation that we be flexible.'

'No, dammit! Those "Redwood Warriors" don't compromise – they wage war and walk away scot-free. I'll be damned if I'll lay down and take the blame!'

Ann nodded. She'd done what she could. The rest was up to the jury.

*

James Pavlik, attorney for the one-armed defendant, was ending his closing argument. 'And in the face of this known risk, not only did Humbolt Logging conduct only a cursory investigation – they also failed to warn the sawmill of a possible threat. Why, ladies and gentlemen, did they act with such callous disregard? because it would have cost them *time and money*.'

Eugene Etter shuffled heavily in his seat but was otherwise silent, expressionless. Pavlik went on:

'Wayne Paul worked on the line in the sawmills for seventeen years. Apart from his service in the Army, it's the only job he'd ever known. It was a hard job but he did it well. And like his father and his grandfather before him, Wayne expected it to be a job for life.' Pavlik looked hard at the jury. 'Ladies and gentlemen, Mr Wayne Paul paid dearly for Humbolt Logging's greed and negligence. He looks to you now for justice.'

There were some cheers for Pavlik when he sat down. A small, noisy clique had positioned itself in the gallery, in the obvious hope of witnessing the disgrace and humiliation of the redwoods' prime enemy – Humbolt Logging. Some of them had tried draping a white banner over the balcony rail, with the message inscribed in blood-red lettering: RED-WOODS YES! LOGGERS NO! – just long enough for the reporters to see it, before Judge Olga Winbush had ordered it removed, threatening to clear the gallery of all spectators.

*

When Ann Kelsey rose to make her closing argument for Eugene Etter, there were some boos for her client, which the judge silenced angrily.

'None of us can imagine,' Ann began, feeling unusually nervous, 'the true horror of sustaining an injury as critical and appalling as Mr Wayne Paul's. But we can sympathise with him as the victim of an unjust and violent accident. Humbolt Logging also sympathise – I promise you that.' More boos. 'Especially since the company has been the frequent and deliberate target of the "Redwood Warriors" destructive, criminal acts.'

At that moment her attention was briefly distracted by the unwelcome sight of Porter Dillon, who had slipped into the side of the court and now stood watching her from just behind counsel's table. Oddly enough, she felt less nervous the moment she saw him. His bright little gloating face only strengthened her resolve. She directed her next words at him, staring him straight in the eyes as she spoke:

'Radical groups like the "Redwood Warriors" freely admit to being saboteurs – advocates of hit-and-run tactics. And true to form, they always vanish before responsibility is addressed.' She paused, trying to eyeball Porter Dillon into looking away, or at least blinking. Instead, he just stood watching her, with a faint smirk on his lips. There was no response from the mob in the gallery.

She went on: 'Mr Etter here has *not* built up a family business with hit-and-run tactics. My client is the only one who sits before you today. And in the absence of the true wrongdoers, the plaintiff hopes you'll find him a convenient scapegoat.'

She paused, and this time she thought she detected Porter Dillon shift uneasily on his feet. He wasn't smiling now. Ann addressed her final words directly to the jury:

'The plaintiff suggests Humbolt Logging acted out of greed. This may be an easy caricature for us to accept. We may even blame loggers for our vanishing forests. We may have already made them fall-guys for our society's own greed – for our insatiable demand for wood and paper. But in suggesting that Humbolt Logging itself acted out of greed, the plaintiff implies that tree-spiking injuries are predictable and commonplace – and therefore somehow acceptable. The truth is, *only one other injury* from tree-spiking has ever been documented. Personal injury from the shattering of a blade against a spike is so uncommon as to be called a freak occurrence. My client took every reasonable step to investigate the warnings he received and he found nothing. He could not have foreseen this accident.' She looked at each of the jury members in turn. 'Ladies and gentlemen, please. Don't compound Mr Paul's tragedy by creating a scapegoat.'

There was dead silence as she resumed her seat. Porter Dillon stood studying the floor in front of him.

Chapter Fifteen

Roxanne stepped out of the lift and stopped dead. Her whole face flushed hot with rage. The reception area of McKenzie Brackman and Partners was seething with technicians, the floor littered with cables, lamps, mobile cameras. She mastered her fury and strode manfully into the chaos, her eyes momentarily dazzled by the glaring white light. A huge sound-boom swung dangerously across the ceiling and a young man with a clipboard shouted, 'Okay, you guys! We'll take the shot with Camera Two racking in from . . .'

Roxanne strode up to him. 'What the hell . . . This is a *law* office!'

The young man glanced at her casually. 'You work here?'

'*Yes I do!* And who gave you permission to come barging in? These are office hours! Who are you, anyway?'

'Assistant Director,' he said, and signalled to someone across the floor. 'Hey, Rick!' he yelled, just loud enough to make himself heard. A second, very suntanned young man with a mane of flowing hair stepped over. He had wrap-around dark glasses and wore a shirt of brown Indian silk hanging loose from his jeans. 'Yeah?' he said, looking at Roxanne. 'Problems?'

'There sure are! What's going on?'

'Some glitch about the office,' the A.D. said.

The second young man stripped off his dark glasses and gave Roxanne a brilliant smile. 'I know we said the office, but maybe we do the first shot here, tracking in from the elevators . . .'

'Who are you?' Roxanne asked icily.

'Rick Nash' – he was smiling with all his teeth now – '"Upside Films". We're doing the location shot for Beauchamp Jeans. This *is* Bloom and Associates – right?'

'This is McKenzie Brackman and Partners. Susan Bloom has an office here.'

'Ah yeah – Susan Bloom. She rented out this location till six a.m. tomorrow morning. We paid eight thousand dollars, and she signed off two weeks ago.' He reached into the back of his jeans and pulled out a thick crumpled contract form.

Roxanne, feeling the rage rising again, brushed past him and managed to locate the receptionist behind the scrum of technicians. 'Get me Susan Bloom. Right away!'

The receptionist smiled. 'She's still in court. On the McArthur Health Shake case. Try tomorrow.'

Roxanne strode back to Rick Nash, slightly spoiling her act by tripping on a cable, and told him, 'Our managing partner isn't here either – and you can't do this without his permission. I'm sure Ms Bloom will refund your money . . .'

'We're talking a lot more than that,' the young man said, beginning to frown. He waved a hand toward the crew. 'These guys are all on the clock and we have heavy equipment rental. If you pull the plug, about thirty grand goes down the drain.' Beside him his A.D. was nodding vigorously.

'If you're saying you're going to sue,' – Roxanne gave a harsh laugh – 'we have the best litigators in town, Mr Nash – right here on the premises!'

'We'd hate to sue,' Nash said, still frowning. 'But we take a big hit if you pull the plug. And we *do* have a signed contract.' He could see she was hesitating; despite her anger, she was thinking of the firm's long-term interests. A law suit brought against them could send the wrong signals.

'If we break or damage anything,' he went on, 'we pay for it.'

Roxanne considered him. He had nice eyes behind the shades, and he seemed anxious and sincere – by L.A. commercial standards. And she thought of Arnie – sweet, reliable, loving Arnie Becker who hadn't addressed a word to her now in two days . . . *Why were men such callous bastards?*

'Okay,' she said, coming down with a bump. 'But just to make sure, I want our security guards here the whole time billed to you.'

'Okay.' Rick Nash visibly relaxed, as he nodded to the assistant director.

'No food, no drinks,' Roxanne went on, 'and no tracking shot through reception. Your contract's for Bloom's office and that's where you stay. If any of the lawyers here complain, we refer them directly to you. And if I even smell you in here after six-oh-one tomorrow morning, we charge another day.'

'Agreed.' He turned to his A.D. 'Let's get to work then.'

'Not so fast!' said Roxanne. 'It's now four-fifty-seven p.m. Your contract says you start at six.' She turned and

153

shouted at the whole crew: 'For the next sixty-three minute
– *nobody moves*!' And she walked purposefully out to he
office. Rick Nash looked annoyed but resigned. He knev
she was the type who meant what she said.

*

'Mr Foreman, has the jury reached a verdict.'

'We have, Your Honour.'

At the tables below, Eugene Etter and Wayne Paul sa
very still. Ann Kelsey crossed her hands in her lap and sai
a little prayer under her breath. Just behind her, in the from
row of the spectators' benches, where she didn't have t
look at him, sat Porter Dillon. He looked smugly expectan

'What say you?' said Judge Olga Winbush.

'In the matter of Paul versus Humbolt Logging,' th
foreman said, 'we find in favour of the plaintiff.'

Against a sustained barrage of applause and cheering
Ann sighed and gave Eugene Etter a short, sorrowful noc
He smiled at her and shrugged.

The foreman of the jury went on: 'And we order th
defendant to pay compensatory damages in the amount c
four hundred and fifty thousand dollars.'

This time Etter frowned and patted her arm: 'Good tr
Ms Kelsey. Could have been a lot worse.'

Judge Winbush was saying: 'Thank you, Ladies an
gentlemen. We're adjourned.'

Meanwhile, Ann Kelsey had become aware of someon
standing at her elbow. It was Porter Dillon; he held out
pale hand but she did not take it. 'Stick around to see bloo
eh?' she said, with contempt.

Porter Dillon chuckled. 'I'm a litigation junkie! I don't admire your politics, Ms Kelsey – but I sure like your work.'

'You don't know anything about my politics,' she said stiffly.

'I know you keep your politics out of your work – and that's a shame.'

'Are you being radical, Mr Dillon, or just plain rude?' When he didn't answer, but just went on smiling, she said, 'You, Snyder and I are all on the same side of the fence. We all want to stop destroying our environment. But you also need to *reach* people with that message – not push them away. If you're so extreme –'

'Yeah, let me guess how it goes,' Porter Dillon sneered. 'We turn people off – give us all a bad name . . .'

'You said it, Mr Dillon.'

'Whereas you, Ms Kelsey, are so darned accommodating, you wind up arguing for the enemy.' He didn't look at Eugene Etter once while he was saying all this, and now turned on his heel and strutted away across the courtroom. Ann Kelsey watched him with plain indifference.

*

Corliss McArthur seemed to fill the whole witness-stand, his extremities bulging loosely over the rails; from the floor of the court he looked like a circus freak, or something out of science fiction. His head was disproportionately small and smooth, like that of a baby. His voice was quiet and high-pitched:

'I've heard all the jokes. '*How d'yer get on Corey's good side?*' Answer: '*Go down three blocks and turn left!*' '*Why*

155

does Corey wear two watches?' 'Because each wrist is in a different time-zone.'

There were titters from round the court, and several jurors had obvious trouble suppressing smiles. Corliss McArthur looked at them pityingly.

'My weight's gone up and down all my life,' he said. 'It took me three years to get it down to one-ninety, and I was determined to keep it that way.'.

'And you thought drinking Mr Kendrick's Health Shakes would help keep it down?' Joe Dumphy asked him.

'That's right. And when I actually started *gaining* weight I told this guy Kendrick my troubles. I thought he was my friend! But here he's pushing me to drink *more*, while all the time he *knows* just how many calories are in that stuff!'

'And how exactly did you discover the truth?' said Dumphy.

'I gave one of those shakes to a nutritionist, and he told meit had over *six-hundred* calories!'

'And you confronted Mr Kendrick?'

'I'm not a violent man, Mr Dumphy. But he provoked me. I tell you, I just – I *snapped. I tell you, Kendrick didn' just ruin my diet – he ruined my life*! After I started bingeing again, I got so fat that my wife found me' – he sniffed back a sob – 'found me sexually undesirable. My marriage collapsed. And all because of *him*!' He nodded tearfully down at the little man, sitting impassively next to Susan Bloom. 'Because of his lies – his fraud! I want him to pay for it!'

Thank you, Mr McArthur. That's all.'

Susan Bloom rose majestically in his place. 'Let me get this straight, Mr McArthur,' she began aggressively. 'You watched my client, Mr Kendrick, add juices, fruit, purée and coconut to your shake – yet you didn't think it might just *add* a few calories?'

'His sign said "as few as seventy calories". That's fraud!'

'Okay,' said Bloom. 'If you see a sale advertising clothes "as low as twenty dollars", do you immediately assume the price of *every* item is twenty dollars?' The fat man swallowed but said nothing. 'You say your marriage broke up as a result of the weight you put on. Isn't it possible that you started putting on weight *because* your wife left you?'

The fat man stared at her, quivering with anger. 'No! No, it is *not*!'

'And you still insist my client is responsible for your weight gain?'

'He is!' Corliss McArthur cried shrilly, 'and he damn well knows it!'

Susan Bloom leant down and collected a sheaf of glossy black-and-white photographs off the table. 'Your Honour, I'd like to introduce these photographs into evidence.' She looked at Corliss McArthur, holding up one of the photos. 'Is this *you*, Sir, on last Thursday night, eating a jumbo pizza-with-everything at Pepe's Pasteria?'

'Objection –' began Dumphy.

'Introducing to impeach, Your Honour,' Bloom said rapidly.

'Overruled.'

Bloom looked hard at the fat man. '*Is* that you, Mr McArthur?' she repeated.

Corliss McArthur gulped but did not reply. Susan Bloom handed the photos to each of the jurors, who eyed them with various degrees of amazement. The fat man observed them miserably, then began: 'I been under a lotta stress – this trial starting . . .'

'And here,' said Bloom, 'three months ago – were you under stress then, when you ordered two buckets of fried chicken, half a dozen biscuits and a tub of coleslaw the size of Coney Island?'

McArthur's fat baby-lips quivered. 'It's called bingeing, Ms Bloom! It's a vicious circle – you get fat, you get depressed, you eat to feel better but it only makes you feel worse, so you eat some *more*!'

'I *know* what it's like, Mr McArthur!' Susan Bloom said triumphantly. 'But no matter how it gets started, don't we all have it in our power to *stop*?' The fat man just stood slumped against the rail, giving no reply.

'Wasn't it your own lack of discipline and willpower,' she went on mercilessly, 'to *lose* that weight that . . .'

'I was like an alcoholic,' the man wailed, 'and *he*' – waving pathetically at Lyle Kendrick – 'he was just shoving the drinks into my hand!'

'Ah come off it, Mr McArthur!' Bloom said savagely. 'You can't face your weight problem, so you have to blame something or somebody else! And this time it happens to be my client, Lyle Kendrick – isn't that it?'

Corliss McArthur just stood, his chins wobbling; then slowly two thick tears began to roll down his fat cheeks.

*

Dr Philip Avery looked like a top adman's dream for a dieting campaign: tall, thin, with dry skeletal features and the bloodless lips of a man who lives off yoghurt and nuts and doesn't drink anything more dangerous than diluted carrot juice.

He was reciting to the Civil Court, in the case of Corliss

McArthur versus Lyle Kendrick, the dismal facts pertaining to over-indulgence in food:

'Over-eating is a disease like alcoholism. If Mr McArthur were fighting to stay sober, and Mr Kendrick had spiked his drinks with liquor, I doubt anyone would blame Mr McArthur for losing control.'

'And, Doctor,' Joe Dumphy asked eagerly, 'what frame of mind would a person have to be in, to do what Mr McArthur did?'

'An obese person's weight is tied to their self-esteem, self-confidence and sexual assurance,' Dr Avery opined sagely. 'When someone promises to help you get slimmer and healthier, but instead makes you heavier – that's traumatic enough. But when it's compounded by that same person calling you a fat pig, or comparing you to Babar the Elephant – well, then you're looking at psychological damage.'

'So it's your opinion that Mr McArthur has suffered as a result?' said Dumphy.

'Absolutely. His self-esteem is at an all-time low. The break-up of his marriage devastated him, and now he's once again trapped in the vicious cycle of bingeing.'

'And you trace this back to what?' Dumphy said.

'To Mr Kendrick's misrepresentations,' the doctor said firmly. 'If it wasn't for him, Corliss McArthur might still be on his diet, and be a happily married man.'

Dumphy was nodding emphatically at this, as Susan Bloom trumpeted: 'Objection, move to strike! Speculative –'

'Sustained,' said Judge Swanson.

'Thank you, Doctor.' Dumphy turned back to the table. 'Nothing more.'

Susan Bloom rose, every ounce of her emanating tense, almost feverish energy. Doctor Avery surveyed her with cool, professional interest, tinged with perhaps a hint of critical disdain.

'If it wasn't for my client,' she began, 'Mr McArthur *might* still be on a diet. Or he might *not*. Right, Doctor?'

'Yes, but . . .'

'So even if my client had never been *born*, Mr McArthur still might've been overwhelmed by the sight of a King Burrito and fallen off the waggon *all by himself*! Isn't that correct?'

'Maybe. But Mr Kendrick's actions virtually assured it. The obese are especially vulnerable to this kind of exploitation.'

'*Really?*' said Bloom. '*All* of us?'

Dr Avery looked vaguely uncomfortable. 'This is all based on demographic studies – profiles . . .'

'Profiles or stereotypes?' Bloom said sharply. 'Are you saying that all fat people are so psychologically unstable that they're moved to physical *assault* more easily than thin people?'

'No. No I'm not. I was talking about Mr McArthur.'

'Oh!' cried Bloom. 'So *he's* unstable?'

'He was provoked,' the doctor said, with just a trace of irritation.

'Psychologically damaged – emotionally devastated . . . He sure sounds unstable to me!' said Bloom.

'Objection!' said Dumphy.

'Sustained.'

'I have nothing further.' Susan Bloom returned to her seat.

It was a mighty crush in the small witness room of the Civil Court. Round the modest table were Susan Bloom, her client Lyle Kendrick, Joe Dumphy, and overwhelming them all – in size, at least – the huge voluminous shape of Corliss McArthur. He was sweating unpleasantly – even the courthouse air-conditioning couldn't cope.

Dumphy, hands on the table, said, 'Okay, here's our offer. You pay fifteen-hundred compensation for the shakes, and thirty-five hundred damages.'

'You're nuts!' cried Kendrick. 'What about *my* damages?'

'I agree,' Susan Bloom said. 'You're in a hole, Joe. I'd rather take our chances with the jury.'

'All right,' said Dumphy, 'three thousand – total.'

Suddenly the fat man turned and faced his attorney. 'No! Stop bargaining. I never want to settle – I let you talk me into this Joe. But I won't sit in here and beg!'

If *I* go on sitting in here, I'm going to pass out! thought Susan Bloom. She said, 'You should reconsider. Joe knows it – I carved up his expert, the doctor.'

'I don't need an expert,' the fat man said, with some dignity. 'I know I'm in the right here.'

'Guess again!' Bloom snarled. 'The jury sees you as a guy carrying a load of emotional problems around – and who wants the whole world to pay . . .'

Corliss McArthur exploded with rage. 'And what about what you carry around, Ms Bloom! What about *your* weight?'

'That's not the issue here,' she retorted.

'The hell it's not!' the fat man yelled. 'You're in denial,

161

lady! You can't admit you got a problem. Instead of dealing with it – instead of losing *your* weight – you beat *me* up!'

'That's garbage!' she snapped.

'Is it? You know exactly what it's like to be me, Ms Bloom. You and I – we have trouble fitting into airplane bathrooms, much less the seat. We go shopping for clothes and get directed to the camping department for a pup tent. People whisper to their kids not to laugh at us.' He gave a deep, baleful sigh.

'You know just how I feel – yet you choose to make jokes about me.' He was met with silence: Susan Bloom, for once, said nothing. 'Whether you like it or not, Ms Bloom,' the fat man added. 'You're one of us. You're just sleeping with the enemy.'

There was silence. Then Corliss McArthur turned and, with a strange dignity, waddled out and headed back to the courtroom. He was followed, at a discreet distance, by a perplexed Joe Dumphy. Susan Bloom just stood and watched; she looked utterly dismayed.

Chapter Sixteen

The man was short, dark, unshaven, in an open-necked shirt and a pair of grubby trousers; on the inside of his hairy arm was the tattooed dagger-symbol of the United States Marine Corps. He sat impassively facing Judge Harlan Shubow, who was presiding over the Los Angeles Criminal Court.

The preliminary hearing was almost over now. The judge said, 'Have we heard statements from all the witnesses?'

Assistant Deputy Attorney Chris Mannen rose; his voice was subdued, resigned: 'Yes, Your Honour.'

'*No, Your Honour!*' a hoarse voice called from the back of the courtroom. A tall, distinguished man with a high domed head came striding down the middle of the courtroom. He looked flushed and out of breath. 'Douglas Brackman,' he said, stopping breathlessly in front of the judge. 'I apologise for being late.'

The A.D.A. stood holding up a sheaf of papers. 'I have Mr Brackman's statement,' he began eagerly.

'All right.' Judge Shubow nodded to Brackman. 'Take the stand.'

The dark unshaven man sat watching Brackman closely;

163

he seemed disappointed by what he saw. The last bandage was gone from Brackman's nose and there was now almost no trace of his recent injuries. Brackman reached the witness stand, took the oath and began to speak. The dark man sat listening carefully, nodding to himself at every sentence, his lips curled into a nasty inane smile.

'And then he proceeded to hit me in the face,' Brackman was saying, 'until I fell to the pavement. Then he kicked me several times in the abdomen before fleeing.'

'Did the assailant speak to you?'

'Yes. He called me a fag and a queer.'

The dark man grinned vigorously at this.

'And what was your reaction to that?' asked the A.D.A.

'I was shocked,' Brackman said, with feeling.

'Because in fact you are not homosexual, are you, Mr Brackman?'

'Because my sexual habits were none of his business,' Brackman said resolutely.

'Did you get a look at your assailant?'

'A very good look.' Brackman turned and looked straight at the dark unshaven man, who stopped smiling now and stared defiantly back. Brackman raised his arm and pointed at him. 'That is the man.'

Judge Shubow began making a note.

'And you'd be able to identify him if he were brought to trial?' asked Mannen.

'I certainly would.' Douglas Brackman had a clear, resolute light in his eyes as he said this; he stood erect, head high, and, for the first time since leaving hospital, the pallor had gone from his face. He was relaxed, at ease with himself, like a man who has suddenly been relieved of a mighty physical burden. He was a man who could look the world in the eye again.

*

In Civil Court Number Two, Joe Dumphy was giving his closing argument for Corliss McArthur. The fat man sat beside him, slumped and motionless, his eyes weary, resigned. It was as though the case had somehow drained all energy from his huge, flaccid body. He might not have lost the case yet, but he had lost weight.

'Lyle Hendrick wasn't just selling health food,' Dumphy was saying. 'He was selling hope. People like him prey on more than their victims' wallets – they prey on their dreams.' He paused, looking slowly across at the jury, then at the plaintiff, Lyle Kendrick, crouched dwarf-like next to Susan Bloom.

'If Mr Kendrick had ripped off old people,' Dumphy went on, 'by promising relief from pain or aging – if he swindled the handicapped, or minorities – there'd be no question about his liability. He'd probably go to jail. But fat people? They're a joke. How can you ever hurt *them*? Well, you can – and he did.' He paused again. Hendrick hunched his head lower, twisted his fingers in his lap.

'Corliss McArthur has a serious illness,' said Dumphy. 'Lyle Kendrick pretended to be his friend – he held out health and hope and the promise of a better life. He betrayed Mr McArthur's trust. And that betrayal, Ladies and gentlemen, should have a price.'

He turned and strode back to his seat.

*

When Susan Bloom rose, she was shaking her head. She looked as though she were about to perform a task she found painful but necessary. 'Ladies and gentlemen of the jury,' she said. 'Lyle Kendrick is not responsible for Corliss McArthur's problems. He's not a therapist – he's not a nutritionist. He's a simple businessman selling his product. And Mr McArthur here chose to buy that product of his own free will. Mr Kendrick *did not* take advantage of him.' She turned and began addressing the whole court, with sudden, genuine passion:

'How dare they! How *dare* they suggest that an entire class of people are more gullible – less able to look out for their own best interests simply because they happen to be *fat*!' She paused to take a deep breath. Her eyes were bright with excitement. 'They want you to believe all fat people are alike. Why? Because then they don't have to deal with us as individuals. They can claim we're all driven by the same demons, that we're all so fragile in our self-image – so *unstable* – that even physical assault, such as the attack on my client, is somehow *justified*!

'Well, ladies and gentlemen, that's hogwash!' – Bloom's voice rose to a harsh crescendo of emotion – 'There are good fat people, there are bad fat people. Sloppy fat people and neat fat people. Well-balanced fat people, and unstable fat people. Corliss McArthur is an unstable man who battered my client. That had nothing to do with his being fat – and if you decide it does, then you diminish us all. Give him – give us all – the respect we're due. Let everybody know that we're ordinary people – not oversized profiles. And that each of us is *different*.'

As she sat down, Joe Dumphy gave a low sigh. *She's good*, he thought. *She's damned good!* They had been two fine closing arguments, he admitted immodestly to himself, and knew the case now balanced on a knife-edge.

*

The interior of Civil Court Number Two was unusually crowded, as the foreman of the jury stood up. A dead silence followed. At last Judge Swanson said, 'Has the jury reached a decision?'

'We have, Your Honour. On the claim of assault and battery, we find for Mr Kendrick' – there were a few cheers and some clapping – 'and order damages in the amount of five thousand dollars.'

In her excitement, Susan Bloom leant over and hugged her client; when she'd finished, the little man had tears in his eyes. But the foreman was not through yet:

'And on the cross-claim of fraud and false advertising, we find for Mr McArthur, and order damages in the amount of five thousand dollars.'

For a moment Corliss McArthur looked stunned, then slowly he began to smile, as the cheering reached him across the courtroom. At the next table, Lyle Kendrick looked more than stunned: the tears had dried even as he was shedding them, and he looked like an angry, bewildered child who's just had an unexpected present snatched away again.

Beside him Susan Bloom was just angry. 'I'll be damned!' she cried.

Judge Swanson gave one of his rare smiles. 'Well. It would seem the Scales of Justice have . . . balanced out. I congratulate the ladies and gentlemen of the jury on a judgement worthy of Solomon himself. Thank you. We're adjourned.'

At the door, pressing their way through the groups of eager spectators and well-wishers, Lyle Kendrick stopped and shook Susan Bloom's hand. 'You were great, Ms Bloom. You made it all worth it – I guess.' He paused; they both turned.

Behind them they saw the gargantuan figure of Corliss McArthur heaving and wobbling towards them like a half deflated barrage balloon being rolled across the floor. He came level with him and stopped, sweating like a sponge. His small watery eyes fixed on Bloom and – ignoring Kendrick entirely – he began to speak, in a low voice quavering with emotion:

'I know you called me "unstable" just now. But all the same, I'd still like to thank you for what you said. Maybe it sounds funny. But you've helped me – a lot.' He suddenly reached out and took her hand in his big pork paw, and shook it, slowly and firmly; then turned and without another word, waddled away.

The woman stood bolted to the floor, staring after him. Corliss McArthur had achieved the impossible. He'd reduced the terrible Susan Bloom to silence.

*

Back at the office Bloom was lying fully stretched on her reclining chair, while a small Hispanic woman stood busily working on her face and neck with a lot of little rubber pads and plastic tubing and wires attached to a metal box that gave off a sinister humming sound.

168

She lay with eyes closed, her black hair encased in a tight-fitting white net. She looked like one of the Pharaohs' aunts being prepared for five thousand years inside a pyramid. From the skin of her face came little popping noises, as the beautician moved the suction pads across Bloom's fat cheeks and over the jowls and folds of her neck.

It was in this inelegant state that Roxanne found the hi-octane lawyer, after walking into her office without knocking. The beautician paused in her work, her slightly Aztec features watching inscrutably, as Roxanne stopped at the chair and glared down at Bloom: 'I want to talk to you. Right now.'

'Honey, it's hard to talk while I'm geting my pores vacuumed.'

'I don't care,' said Roxanne. 'I'm not leaving.' She'd psyched herself up so far for this moment, she darn well meant to go through with it.

Bloom opened her eyes and peered at Roxanne; then wearily sat up and said to the beautician, 'Get yourself some herb tea, baby.'

Roxanne waited till the woman had gone, then exploded: 'You didn't hear a word I said the other day!'

Bloom hauled her stout legs on to the floor and lit a cigarette. She breathed smoke and said, 'We really ought to have that talk about your deal . . .'

'We're having this one first,' said Roxanne, through gritted teeth. 'You said you wanted to be told when you were offensive? Well, renting our firm out as a movie set – *that's* offensive!'

'I said they could shoot in *my* office,' Bloom said calmly. 'Give these producers an inch, they take a mile . . .' She

169

stopped. 'Say, honey – you haven't asked me how my case went today.'

'I'm not interested in your damned case! You're avoiding the issue. You used our place of business like it was a cheap motel room.'

'It was a favour to a friend,' Bloom said airily. 'We set it up days ago and quite frankly – what with this Health Shake case – I forgot. But I was going to give you a percentage . . .'

'Is that what everything is to you – a *percentage*?' Roxanne was in full flood now, and without waiting for a reply, roared on: 'Well, it sure isn't to us! McKenzie Brackman has principles – and you'd better start understanding that! We stand for something in this firm. We don't ambush each other and we don't sell ourselves to the highest bidder!'

'Aw c'mon, Rox. We're talking lawyers here . . .'

'I don't say we're perfect,' Roxanne added. 'But we try to have respect.'

Bloom planted her two feet down on the carpet and leaned forward, drawing deeply on her cigarette. She didn't ask Roxanne to sit down. 'Listen, baby. Let me just tell you about respect. I've had to sweat for it. My family was dirt poor and I went to a little piss-ant college in West Virginia. About a hundred pounds ago, I put myself through law school working as a stripper – and I kid you not! I've taken a lot of crap in my life to get where I am. And I learnt one thing: that "play by the rules" generally means *"pardon us while we screw you"*.'

'You changed the subject,' Roxanne said quietly, but still determined. 'We were talking about how you treat the people you work with.'

Bloom let out an exasperated snort and tossed the half-smoked cigarette into an ashtray big enough to coil a garden hose in. 'God, you don't give up, do you!' She sat up and nodded, 'All right. If I have to be a good little girl, I guess I can handle it.'

'I hope so,' said Roxanne, and turned for the door.

Bloom was suddenly grinning. 'Boy, I can see why they promoted you. You're one hell of a law enforcer!'

Roxanne found herself grinning too, but just managed to get out of the office without showing it. Then she remembered Becker. *Damn Arnie Becker.*

*

The studio lights were on full; the monitors were showing the close of the commercial break. 'Thirty seconds to take . . .!' cried the floor manager. Arnie Becker took a sip of water and calmly straightened his tie. 'How do I look?' he murmured.

'Fabulous.' Julie Rayburn gave him a stunning ear-to-ear smile. 'You've come a long way in five weeks!'

'You really think so?'

'Definitely. You've mastered the art of video foreplay.'

He blinked and stared at her, but she'd turned away. *My God* he thought, *she can't mean what I think she means!* But there was no time for theoretical conjecture. '*Three!* . . . *Two!* . . . *One!* . . .' cried the floor manager. The red light winked on; Julie Rayburn smiled brilliantly into the camera and began:

'We're back, with legal eagle, Arnold Becker.' She turned to him. 'Arnie – what do you say we go back to the phones? We've got time for one more.' She looked at the camera.

'Agnes from City of Industry is on the line. She's got a problem at work.'

'Hi, Agnes.' Becker gave his best bedside smile, resisting the temptation to fiddle with his earpiece. 'I'm Arnie Becker. How can I help you?'

A voice from a dream – a lovely, low, sweet, dangerous voice that somehow combined the caressing tones of Marilyn with the husky lisp of Marlene – filled the crowded studio like a siren-call:

'*Mr Becker, I have a problem at work. I feel like a slave.*'

'I'm sorry to say that's not unusual,' Becker said, in his new T.V.-voice, both urbane and folksy at the same time.

'*My boss keeps giving me more and more work,*' the siren continued. '*Sometimes he threatens me unless I stay late. I don't think he wants me to have any life of my own.*'

Becker looked earnest. 'That's really unfair.'

'*I think so too. I'm trying to take classes, to better myself and all he does is make it harder. Is there anything I can do?*'

Julie Rayburn interrupted, looking at Becker with a mixture of concern and outrage. 'What do you think Arnie?'

Becker furrowed his brow. But he wasn't merely pretending to think: he was doing it for real. For there was something about that voice . . . It wasn't that it was phony or exactly put-on. At least, he didn't think so. But it was vaguely, uncomfortably familiar . . . He said thoughtfully 'Doesn't sound like Agnes's got enough for harassment' – Julie Rayburn looked disappointed – 'but now, if he'd propositioned her . . .'

'*Oh, he's done that,*' Agnes cried, catching them both off guard. '*Several times. He even. . . He seduced me. Once right in the office.*'

172

Julie Rayburn gave a little yell, and Becker said, 'You're kidding.'

'Arnie,' Julie said, 'I certainly hope she can sue this bucket of slime!'

'Absolutely!' he replied, and looked straight at the camera. 'In fact, you've got yourself one *hell* of a lawsuit, Agnes! At the very least, I'd say high six figures.'

'*Wow . . .!*' the voice cooed happily out of the monitors.

'That is,' Becker added solemnly, 'assuming he's got the money. What does this creep do for a living, Agnes?'

'*That's just it. You'd think he'd know better . . . He's a lawyer.*'

Becker gave a start. '*A lawyer . . .!*' He was certain now – he *had* heard that voice before. And recently. But *where*?

'*That's right,*' Agnes purred. '*Somebody that ought to know better than treat a member of his own staff to a one-night stand . . . And in office hours too – in the afternoon, in a crumby downtown hotel . . .*'

'A one-night stand . . . in the afternoon,' Becker repeated, and an awful suspicion began to crawl up the back of his mind.

The voice on the monitors came back, loud and clear: *That's what I said . . . Arnie.*' It was the same voice – only it wasn't Agnes's voice. It was Roxanne's.

He sat paralysed: his concerned lawyer's face frozen rigid with terror. For a moment he just stared into the camera, unable even to move his mouth to speak. He was in a state of panic. He remembered it all now – he and Roxanne lying under the sheet in the little hotel room that afternoon, and now she'd put on that sexy voice, telling him how she'd always wanted to have a 'quickie' with him . . .

He was sweating now, and just hoped the make-up would

173

soak it up. Then suddenly he seized control and began backpedalling desperately: 'Er, Agnes ... I think maybe you should try *talking* to him again.'

'Forget talk,' Julie Rayburn cut in. 'Sue the pig!'

'Can I include pain and suffering?' Roxanne asked, in her natural voice. Becker realised that so obsessed were T.V. people in their own performances, they were impervious to all round them, and that Julie Rayburn had not even noticed the change in the caller's voice. For now he came to think of it, Roxanne's *real* voice was quite sexy. Very sexy, in fact. It was just that he'd known her so long, he'd forgotten to notice it.

'Agnes,' he said, with deep seriousness. 'Let's not be too hasty here. People *can* change. They do change.' Then, hearing the hissing intake of breath from Julie beside him, he began improvising wildly: 'You sound like an exceptionally fair-minded person, Agnes. Why not avoid litigation? Give him one last chance. Negotiate. Maybe you'll get everything you want.'

'*You really think so?*'

'Yes I do. I've got a very good feeling about this. Give it a shot.'

'And if it doesn't work,' Julie Rayburn cut in harshly '*then* sue him.'

Becker nodded vigorously. 'Right.'

'Thanks for the advice, Arnie,' Roxanne said sweetly.

'You're welcome.'

The line went dead. The next moment the floor manager was signalling and the credits began to roll. There was a burst of theme music, and it was the end.

174